THE MELTING CLOCK

The Toby Peters Mysteries

THE MELTING CLOCK

STUART M. KAMINSKY

THE MYSTERIOUS PRESS

New York · Tokyo · Sweden · Milan

Published by Warner Books

 A Time Warner Company

F
KAm

0/0 23 893/

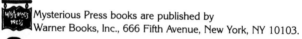 Mysterious Press books are published by
Warner Books, Inc., 666 Fifth Avenue, New York, NY 10103.

 A Time Warner Company

The Mysterious Press name and logo are trademarks of Warner Books, Inc.
Printed in the United States of America
First Printing: December 1991

10 9 8 7 6 5 4 3 2

Library of Congress Cataloging-in-Publication Data

Kaminsky, Stuart M.
    The melting clock / Stuart M. Kaminsky.
        p.   cm.
    ISBN 0-89296-435-9
    I. Title.
    PS3561.A43M44   1991
    813'.54—dc20
                                                            91-50203
                                                               CIP

To our good friends Carol Johnson and Richard Lilly
on the *Peniche Astrolabe*

The secret lies in lucidly keeping a steady course between the waves of madness and the straight lines of logic.

—Salvador Dali

1

"Grasshoppers," Salvador Dali whispered, shrinking back as I opened the door. He didn't say "grasshoppers" exactly, it was more like "grah-zoppairs," but I understood the word as he repeated it, his eyes open wide, his long, dark waxed mustaches curled upward at the end like sharp-pointed black surgical needles.

"A giant monk with an ax is coming through that door behind you in about ten seconds," I said.

The door I was pointing to shuddered.

"Make that five, Sal. What'll it be, a couple of grasshoppers outside or a split personality?"

Dali, dressed in a white rabbit suit, removed the deerstalker hat perched on his head and pointed at the splintering door with one hand. Then he did a little dance from foot to foot as if he had to find a toilet.

It wasn't much of a room, a couple of mismatched chairs with a small round table between them. A table-top Philco radio was on and Martha Tilton was singing

"From Taps Till I Hear Reveille." The room looked as if it were set up for a seance or a sanctuary to worship the Blue Network. The room did have one thing going for it—a big window through which, by the light of the full moon and about forty yards away down the hill, I could see a party going on. Beyond the party, I could see the Pacific Ocean.

We were in Carmel, the house Dali and Gala were renting for the duration of the war. We'd just finished a whirlwind tour of the place. It had had to be quick. The ax wielder kept cutting it short.

"No, no, no, no," Dali had shouted three rooms and a century ago, "Not the fish room." We had run through an area apparently intended to comprise the living room. It had deep, overstuffed blue furniture, pale blue walls. On one wall a big fat blue fish was painted. The fish had been smiling.

As we stood now, only one door between us and the pebbled driveway where my Crosley was waiting to rescue us, a panicked Dali repeated "Grasshoppers" once more, emphatically, as if I were the town idiot who couldn't understand that the possibility of encountering a grasshopper ranked right up there with being on the ground at Hickem Field when the Japanese hit Pearl Harbor.

The head of the monk's ax hit the door behind us again and went through, sending a hefty splinter flying over Dali's shoulder. The chunk of wood landed in my quiver of arrows. Bull's-eye.

"We go," said Dali, dashing past me to open the door to the grounds.

Once outside, Dali exploded in hysteria, and I looked back to see the head of the ax back out of the hole through which I could now see the monk's robe and black hood.

I followed Dali and kicked the door shut behind us.

There was enough light from the windows in the room behind us for me to see Dali's Sherlock Bunny face as he stood frozen, his eyes on the ground in front of us searching for the dreaded . . .

"Grasshoppers," he gasped.

The giant behind us took another whack at the interior door. I heard a hinge give. I thought. My Crosley was about twenty yards away. Dali's nearest neighbor was about half a mile away. I was no more than five-nine and 160 pounds on a good day. Dali was at least two inches shorter and no more than 130 pounds tops, even with the rabbit suit. But Dali was about forty, and I was looking at half a century in the calendar. Besides, I was recovering from a recently broken leg.

"I'm not carrying you," I said, moving toward my car.

"Listen," Dali whispered grabbing my sleeve.

"Grasshoppers, crickets, a bunch of tree frogs. Can we continue our nature studies in the car?"

A breeze came up from the ocean and billowed Dali's loose white fur. It might have been kind of cute if an ax hadn't just destroyed what remained of the inside door.

The hell with it. I picked Dali up in my arms like a baby and staggered to the Crosley. My back would make me pay for this later, but so would Dali if I lived to send him a bill and he lived to pay it. I could smell Dali's mustache wax and hair cream. It's Jarvis, I thought, putting him down near the passenger door. He didn't want to go down but he didn't have a choice. Somewhere between the house and the car he had lost the deer-stalker and his slicked-back hair had started to rise like a frightened character in a Popeye cartoon. He let out a squeak appropriate to his costume and reached for the door. I grabbed his hand.

"Driver's door's broken, remember?" I said.

"No," Dali squealed.

I didn't answer. I pushed past him and did the twists

and turns to get myself into the driver's seat. Since the Crosley was only a little bigger than one of those midget cars the clowns squeeze into in the circus, it was no mean trick, especially with Dali almost on my back.

The unlocked back door of the house crashed open and a dull orange bolt of light came through the dirty rear windows of my car. Dali hyperventilated at my side as I reached for the ignition. The key was still where I'd left it. Fortunately, the monk with the ax was no Clifton Fadiman.

I turned the key. Nothing.

The orange bolt dulled with the approaching shadow of the mad monk.

"*Vehemence,*" said Dali, looking back over his shoulder. "*Patti, avant, go.*"

"It won't go," I said.

"Dali says it must go," he demanded, holding up a single finger before my face as if he were a scolding teacher and I was the class dunce.

"It won't go," I repeated.

"Shoot him, Peters," Dali demanded as the ax wielder moved in front of the Crosley.

"My gun's broken," I said.

"Then, then . . ." Dali stammered.

"Yeah," I agreed.

"This is not happening to Dali," he said, closing his eyes. "Where is Gala? She must do something."

Since his wife was on the beach, surrounded by people in idiotic costumes, I didn't think we had much chance of hearing from her in the next fifteen seconds. There was no way I could get past Dali and out the passenger door in time. I wouldn't be able to run.

While I was considering all this, the ax blade came down on the hood of the Crosley about a foot from my face. Metal clanked against metal and the blade bit into the tinfoil hood of the car. Dali tried to climb backward over his seat but there was nowhere to go. The blade came out with the screech of a demon's fingernail across a black heart.

The monk stepped back and looked from Dali to me, deciding who should lose his head first. I lost. The monk started around to my side of the car.

"Open the door," I whispered. "And run like hell. Get help."

The ax scratched across my window and I thought I saw a grin in the darkness of the hood. I didn't grin back.

"Now," I told Dali.

"No," he said, behind me.

"Why?"

"Grasshoppers," he whispered.

2

It all started that Friday, New Year's Day, 1943. Well, at least the year started that Friday. The things that led to me being nose-to-nose with an ax-carrying lunatic through the not-very-thick glass of my car window probably began when we were both born. Maybe a hell of a lot earlier.

It was sometime in the afternoon at Mrs. Plaut's boarding house on Heliotrope in a not-so-bad area of Los Angeles not far from downtown. Mrs. Plaut had thrown a wild party the night before to welcome in the new year. To celebrate the occasion, she had put together a dress that looked like a shroud with lunatic flowers of every shape and color sewn onto it. There was very little of her in the first place. Eighty years of life had eroded her into a tough hickory cane lost in the enormity of that dress, the construction of which she had badly miscalculated, probably based on memories of a more matronly body.

Highlights of the Plaut festivities, in order, were:

- Mr. Hill, the mailman, his unnecessarily tight tie threatening to strangle him, singing a medley of songs starting with "Cupid's Stupid Isn't He?" and ending with, "The Donkey Serenade."
- Mrs. Plaut's elderberry punch, made from elderberry *saft* sold by her nephew Ridgeway, a traveling salesman who appeared for about half an hour about once a year looking back over his shoulder for dissatisfied customers or ex-wives.
- Guy Lombardo on the radio from 11:30 P.M. till midnight, when we sang "Auld Lang Syne."

When Carmen Lombardo sang "and never brought to mind," I thought I saw a tear in the corner of the eye of Gunther Wherthman, my best friend, who lives in the room next door to mine, and who also happens to be three feet tall and Swiss. Gunther had brought a date to the festivities, a graduate student in music history named Gwen, whom we had met on a case in San Francisco two months before. Gwen looked on Gunther with adoration, seeing only a gentle man who spoke and wrote eight languages and knew the difference between a woman and a lady. Gwen looked a bit more like a toothpick than a woman or a lady, but Gunther saw only the adoration.

I had asked Anne, my former wife, to spend New Year's Eve with me but she'd said she had to stay home and do her nails instead. I had a feeling she was doing more than her nails. I tried Carmen, the cashier at Levy's, but the ample Carmen had said she'd promised her son that she'd be with him New Year's Eve.

"You wanna come?" she had asked without enthusiasm as she rang up my Reuben and Pepsi. "We're gonna toast marshmallows and stuff."

"What stuff are you going to toast?" I'd asked.

"Just stuff," she said.

That had been the second-longest conversation I had ever had with Carmen. The longest one had been about Roy Rogers.

So, I had decided to stay home and join the Plaut New Year's Eve party. I should have gone to Carmen's house to toast stuff.

Mrs. Plaut had concluded New Year's Eve with the reading of a passage about her Cousin Ardis Clickman, from her massive memoirs. I was editing her memoirs. At various times Mrs. Plaut thought I was an exterminator, then a book editor. I don't know how she'd come to either conclusion. Many have tried to penetrate Mrs. Plaut's fantasies. All have failed. I had long since given up telling her that my name was and is Peters, Toby Peters, private investigator, not exterminator, not editor.

"Mr. Peelers," she said on that semi-sultry Los Angeles night, "you need pay special attention since you will get my inflection which is not available to you when you are at the task of editing the Plaut saga."

"I'll pay special attention," I had promised.

I looked at her bird, whose name changed at Mrs. Plaut's whim. From the perch in his cage, Carlyle—or was his name now Emmett?—cocked his head to one side and contemplated the tale Mrs. Plaut monotoned for almost an hour.

It had to do with "The Mister" who, along with Uncle John Anthony Plaut and Aunt Claudia had, on New Year's Night, 1871, decided to attack the local settlement of Pawnees—always good fun when one grew weary of watching the fire crackle and re-reading *Goody's Journal.*

It seems that "The Mister," who would later marry

Mrs. Plaut when he was ancient and she was a child, was particularly fond of the Pawnees. Since I valued my sanity more than my curiosity, I didn't bother to question this. I doubt if Mr. Hill even heard it. His eyes indicated that, inspired by elderberry punch, he was off to undreamed of ports of call. No, it was Gwen, who took things and people at their word, who asked the question,

"Why did they want to attack the Pawnees?"

"One may like a class of human species and still feel the necessity of causing their demise for reasons to do with survival and such like," Mrs. Plaut explained, patiently.

"Well," I said when I thought she had finished her tale. "This was some party, but I've got to get up early."

"I've never known a man to refuse a final cup of Grandmother's elderberry punch," she said, evening up the pages of the hand-written manuscript. Over the years, the thing had grown to massive proportions.

"I must," I said sadly.

Mrs. Plaut placed her manuscript back in the linen-covered box from whence it had come and handed it to me.

"I think it's time I took Gwen home," said Gunther, jumping down from the sofa with practiced dignity and offering his hand to his date. He was the only one dressed for the occasion, complete with three-piece suit and tie with a matching handkerchief in the jacket pocket.

Mr. Hill, if his face was a reasonable window to his soul, was over the sea in Erin, dreaming of Leprechauns.

And that was it.

I wished everyone a happy New Year and went to the pay phone on the second-floor landing. I dropped in a nickel and called Anne. She answered on the first ring.

"Hello," she said in the voice that never failed to stir memories.

"Annie, Annie was the miller's daughter," I recited. "Far she wandered from the singing waters. Up hill, down hill Annie went a maying . . ."

"Toby, I was in bed."

"Happy New Year," I said. "You want me to come over?"

"No," she said.

"I'm sober," I said.

"I can tell. You never were much of a drinker, even on New Year's Eve."

"I've had a depressing night," I said.

"So you'd like to come over and depress me?"

"That was not my plan."

"You didn't have a plan, Toby," she said quietly. "You never have a plan."

And then I heard it—something, someone.

"You're not alone," I said.

She said nothing.

"I'm sorry," I said.

"You couldn't know," Anne said gently.

"No, I'm sorry you're not alone."

"I hope you have a good new year, Toby," she said.

"Yeah." I hung up, imagining Anne who, at forty-one, was dark, full, and might be considering her third husband. I had been the first. Ralph, the second husband, was another story.

There was only one other person to call. I did it. A girl answered.

"Who's this?" I asked.

"Tina Swerler," she said. "The babysitter. The Pevsners are out. It's after midnight."

"Did I wake up the kids?"

"Lucy and Dave are asleep. Nat's still up."

"Can I talk to him?"

Pause and then, "Uncle Toby?"

"Yeah."

"You on a case?"

"Yeah," I said.

Nat was twelve. He knew better than to ask me if I'd killed anyone today. That was David's question. David was eight and kept track of my murders in the pursuit of justice. The last time I had checked with David the count was sixteen. I was still well behind David Harding, Counterspy. The truth was I'd never killed anyone, and had only shot in the general direction of a few people in the ten years since I'd left the Glendale Police Department. I was and am a terrible shot.

"Tina let me taste wine," Nat said.

"How old is Tina?" I asked.

"Seventeen," he said.

"Tell your father and mother I said happy New Year. And tell David and Lucy. I'll try to stop by tomorrow."

"You mean later," he corrected me. "It's already tomorrow."

"It's never tomorrow," I corrected him.

"I guess," he replied, perplexed. "Are you drunk, Uncle Toby?"

"Not yet," I said. "Good-night, kid."

"Good-night, Uncle Toby. Uncle Toby?"

"Yeah, Nat."

"He doesn't want to be called David, or even Dave. He wants to be called Durango."

"Durango Pevsner," I said. "I'll try to remember. Thanks. Good-night."

There was no one else to call. I wouldn't go to Phil's house in the morning. I didn't know why. I just knew I wouldn't go. I'd stay in my room till I went nuts. Then I'd go to my office or to a movie. Usually I could count on Gunther to accompany me to nearly any movie, but Gunther now had Gwen.

I went into the bathroom I shared with Mr. Hill and Gunther, put Mrs. Plaut's manuscript on the sink and looked at my face in the mirror. I had shaved before the party but I still didn't look like Victor Mature. The hair was there and dark, mainly, with flecks of gray. The nose was flat and the eyes brown. The ears stuck out a little, which should have detracted from the image of the guy who shouldn't be messed with, the guy who knows how to take a punch and how to give one. Only I hadn't given many punches.

I had a good face for my profession. Maybe I should have been better at it, but I lacked ambition. That was what Anne had always said, that I lacked ambition and was still about fourteen years old emotionally.

Who the hell was Anne with tonight? No, don't think that way. Next thing you know you'll be listening in on phone calls, going through her garbage for notes, taking photographs from trees, and following her around to girdle shops.

I went back to my room. My room at Mrs. Plaut's was modest. Sofa with doilies made by the great lady herself, complete with a small purple pillow on which was sewn "God Bless Us Every One." On the wall was a Beech-Nut Gum clock that told pretty good time, at least as compared to my watch. I took the watch off and put it on the little dresser near the door. It had been my father's, the only thing he had left me. It told the right time twice a day if I was lucky and didn't rewind it.

I had a bed, but I didn't use it much. I dragged the mattress onto the floor to appease the God of Bad Backs. There were a few Gobel beers in the small refrigerator in the corner. They'd been there for months. I fished behind the milk and found one. I pulled it out, closed the door, sat at my little table for two, and popped the top with my Pepsi opener.

I didn't want a beer, but I drank it. I owed it to Nat.

With Mrs. Plaut's chapter at my side, I lay on the

mattress and was asleep on the floor in my underwear before the Beech-Nut Gum clock clicked to one.

When I woke up in the morning, the cat was sleeping on the bed next to me.

The cat's name is Dash. Notice I didn't say "My cat's name is Dash." He's not mine. He abides with me when he wants to come in through the window, get some attention, and eat. He's big and orange and saved my life once.

I made the dangerous barefooted journey to the front porch in my blue beach robe that had *Downtown Y.M.C.A.* written on the back in black letters. I almost never beat Mrs. Plaut to the *L.A. Times*, but she must have slept in after a party that rivaled those thrown by John Barrymore and Fatty Arbuckle.

Back in my room, I fixed myself a bowl of Wheaties and a glass of Borden's Hemo, did the same for Dash, and read the paper while I ate. I considered a second round for both me and the cat, but milk was up to fifteen cents a quart and clients were down almost one hundred percent.

My back was okay and I wasn't feeling as sorry for myself as I had the night before, partly because the sun was bright, partly because it was a new year and the news wasn't bad.

The Soviets were routing the Nazis, claiming that more than 312,000 Germans had been killed. Even Hitler was telling the Germans that it was going to be a tough year. And here at home, oleomargarine was hard to get.

In the movie section I found two choices, either *Who Done It?* with Abbott and Costello or *Time to Kill* with Lloyd Nolan as Mike Shayne. Tough choice. I decided on both of them, providing the Rose Bowl game was over early enough. I had a busy day planned.

I lay in bed grappling with Mrs. Plaut's prose until the

game came on. The *Times* had reported that Georgia coach Wally Butts had said Frank Sinkwich wouldn't start. His star running back had a bad ankle. Sophomore Charlie Trippi would replace him. Trippi was supposed to be okay, but no offensive match for U.C.L.A. quarterback Bob Waterfield's arm.

I slept on and off through most of the game and woke up when the crowd, reported at 93,000, roared and I heard a voice say that Sinkwich had gone in for the touchdown. Dash didn't seem to be around.

"Telephone," came Mrs. Plaut's voice from outside my door.

I mumbled some dry-mouthed something that I hoped would satisfy her and let her know I was trying to rejoin the land of the living, but Mrs. Plaut was not an easy woman to reach. She came through the door and looked down at me. She was wearing what at first looked like a cloak and dagger but turned out to be a U.C.L.A. shawl and trowel.

"Telephone," she repeated.

"Mrs. Plaut, though I know this will do me no good, to hold onto the illusion that you and I are capable of communication, I'll ask you again, please don't come in here without the following scenario: You knock and I answer. I answer one of several ways: Come in. Just a minute. Or, I can't open the door now. There are variations on this."

"Phone is waiting," she said, looking first at me and then at the crumpled *L.A. Times*, "and I've got apples to peel."

"I'm almost naked," I said, sitting up.

"You are just noticing that?" she asked. "I knew it as soon as I came through the door. Kindly put the newspaper back together, especially the funny papers and the cooking, and bring it down to me."

"Who . . ?" I began, but she was gone.

I put on my blue robe and went out to the phone on the landing. "Hello," I said.

"Dali is distraught," came a high-pitched woman's voice with a distinct accent that might have been Russian.

"Sorry to hear that," I said.

"When Dali is distraught, he cannot work," she went on. "He can think only brown. Brown is not a good color for Dali to think in."

"I see," I said. Downstairs, Mrs. Plaut carried a bowl of apples out onto the front porch.

"Only Dali truly sees," she said.

"What are we talking about?" I asked.

"You did not answer Dali's letter."

Then it hit me. A few weeks ago when I was lying on the mattress in broken-legged pain, Mrs. Plaut had handed me a pink envelope with an eye painted on it. She told me that the letter had been delivered by a woman in a funny hat.

"You're the woman in the funny hat," I said.

"I am Gala, the wife of Dali, formerly Gala Eluard, born Elena Deluvina Diakonoff."

I considered asking her what the next race she was running in was, now that I knew her lineage, but I sometimes remember what side my bread is margarined on.

"What can I do for you?" I asked amiably, smelling insanity or a client or both. I have taken money from both the guilty and the insane. With the price of milk going up and margarine as hard to get as gas coupons, a man in my business took what he could get. Shoplifter patrol at the neighborhood Ralph's Grocery was the only work I'd done for the past two weeks.

"You read Dali's letter?"

I had read it. I still had it in the second drawer of my dresser. It said:

I cannot understand why man should be capable of so little fantasy. I do not understand why, when I ask for a grilled lobster in a restaurant, I am never served a cooked telephone; I do not understand why champagne is always chilled, and why on the other hand telephones, which are habitually so frightfully warm and so disagreeably sticky to the touch, are not also put in silver buckets with crushed ice around them. Please try to locate a telephone which does not offend you and call me at the number below. I am in need of your services.

"I called the number in the letter," I said. "It was a Greek bakery."

"Impossible," she said. "Dali does not like Greek pastry. The dough is like gritty paper covered in honey."

"I can't argue with that," I said, "but it was a Greek bakery."

"There are no Greek bakeries in Carmel," Gala Dali said triumphantly.

"Well, you got me there. Yes, ma'am. But I called a Los Angeles number."

"We are in Carmel," she said.

"The letter didn't say that."

"Everyone knows Dali is in Carmel," she admonished.

Although I was living proof that this was not so, I had no desire to prolong the discussion or provoke a possible client. I said nothing and after about five seconds she seemed to accept that as an apology.

"Are you available?" she said. "We must—"

Someone interrupted her in a foreign language and she answered. They went back and forth for a few seconds while I waited, wondering if I could still catch the Abbott and Costello movie or give up and listen to the Philco special, "Our Secret Weapon." Rex Stout was going to expose Axis lies. Dash and I could curl up with some bran flakes and give our moral support to the Allies.

Gala came back on the line.

"Dali wants to know if you have blue eyes."

"Brown," I said.

More discussion in a foreign language.

"That is acceptable. Are you a Surrealist?"

"I'm a private detective," I said patiently.

Then a man's voice came on the phone, excited, so accented that I could barely understand what was being said.

"I do not deal with Breton and his Surrealists. Do you know why?"

"They don't shower regularly."

"No, I do not know if they shower regularly. The difference between me and the Surrealists is that I am a surrealist."

"I'll remember that."

The woman was back on the line now.

"Dali is upset."

"I could tell. I'm a detective."

"We must see you. We have lost weeks."

"Why me?"

"Poldi," she said.

"Poldi?"

"Stokowski, Leopold Stokowski," she explained impatiently. "You worked for him. He told us you could help. Someone has stolen three of Dali's paintings and three clocks, clocks my mother gave to me, the only things I have from Russia, from Dr. Lazovert in St. Petersburg when we—"

"I'm sure you considered this, but how about the police?"

"No, no, no, no, no, no," she said and Dali took the phone from her to add, "No, no, no, no, no."

And then she was back.

"There are things . . . there is something in one of the paintings that must never be seen by the public. The paintings were taken from our house. They were not meant to be seen. The shock would . . . it would be . . ."

She couldn't imagine what it would be and neither could I. I didn't know much about Dali. I knew he was Spanish, read that he was a bit nuts or putting on a show that he was nuts to sell his paintings. This was the Salvador Dali who painted men with shit on their pants, painted old men with erections that looked like melting pianos, and designed hats with figures of dead babies on them. This was the guy who said his plan was to shock the world every twenty-four hours. What the hell could he have painted that he thought the world couldn't handle?

" . . . shocking," I said.

"Shocking, yes. We have had a message from the thief," she said. "I must read it to you."

"Let's talk business first," I said.

"They have not indicated what they want," she replied.

"No, let's talk about my business. Twenty dollars a day, plus expenses, plus one original painting by Dali if I get any of the paintings back."

"The money is nothing," she said, "but you are asking for a Dali painting, a piece of his soul."

"A small piece will be okay. And he turns them out fast," I said.

She passed the terms on to Dali and came back on the line to say, "Yes."

"One hundred dollars in advance when I get to Carmel," I prompted.

"We are not in Carmel now," she said. "The thief said he was in Los Angeles. We came in a limousine. We are in the Beverly Hills, the home of a friend. You must come now."

She gave me an address on Lomitas; I told her I'd change and be there in about an hour.

"One hundred dollars when I get there," I reminded her.

"Yes, yes," she agreed and hung up.

I went back to my room, wrote the address in my battered spiral notebook, and got dressed, pleased with myself that I'd added the painting into my fee. I'd never seen one of Dali's paintings. Didn't think I'd like them from the descriptions I'd read, but it would be something Jeremy Butler might want. Jeremy was the landlord at the Farraday Building, where I had an office inside the office of Sheldon Minck, D.D.S. Jeremy, large, bald, somewhere in his sixties, had made a few dollars as a pro wrestler and invested the dollars in a downtown office building on Hoover, as well as various other properties around town. His specialty was taking buildings on the way down and using his muscle and will power to embarrass them and make them respectable and profitable. I had the feeling he hadn't been particularly successful. But Jeremy was a poet, a poet who had recently married and fathered a remarkably beautiful round baby named Natasha. The Dali would be a gift for Natasha, if I got the paintings back.

I put on the best of what I had left in the closet. I didn't have a clean suit or a sports jacket. I didn't really have dirty ones either. A suitable addition to my wardrobe was high on the list of purchases planned for Dali's advance money. I did have a windbreaker: showerproof, gabardine, brown, and lined with rayon. Zipper pocket over the left breast and reasonably clean. I'd picked it up new for eight bucks at Hy's for Him. My underwear was

passable, my socks dark, my trousers only slightly wrinkled and blue enough to hide any stains I didn't want to
investigate. It was the best I could do.

I dragged the mattress back on the bed, sort of straightened the covers and watched Dash crawl out from under
the sofa and stretch. I gave him a few seconds to figure
out where he was and then picked him up and tucked
him under one arm. Mrs. Plaut's manuscript was under
the other.

I didn't expect to avoid Mrs. Plaut. I didn't even try.
She sat peeling apples on the white-painted front porch
swing, watching the neighbors when they appeared. I
dropped Dash on the porch and he went down the stairs
and out of sight into the bushes.

"That was some party," I said, putting the manuscript
box next to Mrs. Plaut on the swing.

"What do you think about kindergarten, Mr. Peelers?"
she asked as I brushed orange cat hairs from my windbreaker.

"I don't remember it well, Mrs. Plaut," I said. "I do
remember Evelyn Yollin, the shortest girl in class,
who—"

"No," she interrupted when I had almost retrieved the
image of little Evelyn, who might be a grandmother
now. "Uncle Robert's idea about kindergarten."

I hadn't read most of Mrs. Plaut's chapter but I'd
scanned it and didn't remember an Uncle Robert. She
looked up into my bewildered face.

"Not my Uncle Robert from Port Arthur, the radio
Uncle Robert in New York who says we should get rid of
the word *kindergarten* because it's a German word."

"Ah," I said. "I haven't really—"

"Nonsense," she said, looking over the roofs across the
street toward the eastern sky. "Plaut is a German name.
What would they call kindergarten? What would they
call Plaut?"

"I don't know," I said.

"Radio people, painters, and the emperor of Japan are crazy people," she said, returning to her apples. "I'm going to make Apples Eisenhower. Eisenhower is a German name, too. If you do not come back before three hours it will be ready and you may have some. I cannot prevent you from giving some to the orange cat, but I would prefer that you not give him much. He's beginning to look sassy though he no longer looks with hunger at my bird."

"I'll ration his Apples Eisenhower," I promised.

"Speaking of rations," she said. "Stamp number twenty-four in War Ration Book One is good for one pound of coffee until January twenty-one. Sugar stamp number ten in War Ration Book One is good for three pounds of sugar until January fifteen. Gasoline A coupon number four is good until January twenty-one. Stamp number seventeen in War Ration Book One is good for one pair of shoes until June fifteen."

I didn't ask how she remembered all of this. I just said, "You can have them all, Mrs. Plaut."

She nodded and went on, "Blue A, B, and C stamps in War Ration Book Two will be issued in February. They are worth forty-eight points worth of canned and other processed foods for the month of March."

"You may have them all, Mrs. Plaut."

"War is hell, Mr. Peelers."

"I've got to go, Mrs. Plaut. Dali's expecting me."

"The one from Tibet," she said knowingly.

I'd been through this with her before so I said, "Yes, Mrs. Plaut."

"Book or pests?" she asked.

It took me a beat to understand. "No, he hasn't written a book and he doesn't need an exterminator."

"Ah," she said with a very knowing smile. "They're wrong about the kindergarten thing, you know."

"They're wrong," I agreed. "I'll see you later."

My khaki-colored Crosley was, as all Crosleys are, almost small enough to pick up and carry under one arm. I'd bought mine used from No-Neck Arnie the mechanic for two hundred dollars. He'd got it from a guy who'd picked it up at a hardware store in 1940. It wasn't a bad car. Maybe the reason it didn't catch on was the brilliant marketing idea of selling them in hardware and appliance stores like ladders and coping saws.

I was feeling pretty good when I turned the corner at Heliotrope and drove over to Arlington to head north. Crossing the street when I got to Arlington were a man and a woman. The woman looked like Anne. I drove past and looked back. It wasn't Anne.

I had paid No-Neck Arnie fifteen bucks to install a radio in the Crosley. Crosleys came without frills—just a speedometer, a fuel gauge, and a water gauge, but I needed company when I drove. One of the Eberle brothers was singing "This Love of Mine." I turned the radio off and paid attention to the road.

3

T he address wasn't hard to find. It was set in white stones on a black marble slab. The house itself, a big brick English-looking thing with slanted red roofs set back about a hundred yards from the street on a paved driveway, couldn't be seen through the small forest of trees in front of it. Since there weren't any guards, walls, or gates, whoever owned it probably wasn't in the movies or the rackets.

There were two cars in the driveway, though I could see a garage at the side of the house with its doors up and enough room for the Beverly Hills fire department. Inside the garage a man with his back to the driveway was washing a car the size of Hoover Dam and the color of a robin's egg. I parked behind a white 1941 Lincoln convertible with its top down. Parked in front of the Lincoln was something I'd never seen before.

I walked over to look at it and still didn't know what I was looking at. It looked a little like a Cord but . . .

"It's a Hupmobile," came a voice behind me.

25

The guy was about forty, tall, thin, a lopsided Henry Fonda type, only older with graying temples. He was wearing grease-smeared overalls. His hair flowed forward, almost covering his eyes. A spot of oil in the shape of a lima bean smudged his cheek. He was wiping his hands with a once-white rag.

"Only three hundred nineteen of them made," he said. "Got it for less than eleven hundred. Keep it in shape, it should be worth forty or fifty thousand in twenty years. Should have bought a dozen of them but where would I put them?"

He looked around and it seemed to me he had enough room for at least twenty-five or thirty of the Hups.

He held out his hand and I took it. The grip was firm and the smile sincere.

"Barry T. Zeman," he said.

"Toby Peters," I said.

"That automobile J.T. is working on," he said, nodding toward the blue Hoover Dammobile. "A 1940 Cadillac Fleetwood Series town car."

"Looks great."

"Take care of that Crosley of yours and it'll be worth something in twenty years," he said, nodding at my car.

"I need it for transportation," I said.

"The future," he said, pushing his unruly hair back. "That's where I live. That's how I made my money."

"The present," I said. "That's where I live and why I don't have any money. This is your place?"

"My place, and my wife's. You're the detective."

"I'm the detective," I admitted, following him up the stone walk to the front door, which opened suddenly. A woman the size of Alaska stepped out, closed the door, and looked over our heads down the driveway. Her yellow-white hair was bun-tight and her cloth coat was open, revealing a serious white uniform. I glanced back over my shoulder to the driveway, where a cab was pulling up. Zeman and I parted so the woman could get through.

He leaned back in. "Find the paintings and the clocks or tell them as soon as you can that you can't do it," he said softly. "I'll give you five hundred cash if this is all over either way in two days."

Behind us the cab door opened and closed and, a beat later as Zeman opened his front door, the cab took off.

"Five hundred," he repeated. "I've got an investment in Salvador Dali. Quite a collection, thirty paintings, drawings, and even some jewelry and sculpture. You'll see it inside. Know what it'll be worth in twenty years?"

"As much as a Hupmobile," I guessed.

"Much more," he said with a grin. "I've got an investment in the man, an investment for me, my kids, my grandchildren. I'll be nice to him. That's business, but I tell you, Toby, between the two of them, they drive me and the wife crazy nuts. Wife's taken off for Palm Springs till they go. I'm a prisoner of my investments."

"I'll do my best to wrap this up in two days," I said, "but . . ."

He pulled a business card from the pocket in the bib of his overalls and handed it to me. It had a little thumb print on it and an address and phone number on Sunset Boulevard. Mr. Zeman's line of business was printed under his name: *Investments*. I unzipped my windbreaker pocket, tucked the card away, and zipped up again as Zeman opened the door and let me in.

The living room into which we walked was bright and big, white walls to a skylight in the ceiling. The furniture was all modern, whites and blacks with hardwood floors and colorful patterned rugs.

"Decorated by Dali himself to show off the paintings," said Zeman, folding his hands behind him as I looked around at the walls and the seven pictures hung there. They were all different sizes. The smallest was a black-and-white study of an egg on a seashore. Something had pecked through the egg and was trying to get out, something with a beak and a human arm. The painting was about the size of the cover of an atlas.

There were bigger ones, some of them filled with little objects, all of them colorful. Seashores or deserts with long pianos on the beach and old men with huge behinds hovering over girls. Seashells and limp things that shouldn't be limp, books, shells, pianos, radios, watches. They looked like they were melting from the heat. A grasshopper sat on the shoulder of a woman who was kissing a tall man. From the angle you couldn't be sure whether he was, in fact, kissing her or the grasshopper.

"Response?" asked Zeman, beside me.

"I don't know. Strong. Hard to look away from. Sad, maybe."

"Dali's paintings are not sad," came a woman's accented voice, the voice I had heard an hour earlier on the phone. "Dali's paintings are a celebration of the inner voice. He doesn't not paint what other people see. He paints what no one sees."

"I'll go with that," I said, looking at her.

She was small and clearly the boss wherever she went. She moved past Zeman into the middle of the room and looked around at the paintings.

"That," she said, pointing at the largest one above a white sofa, "is me."

She was right. It was Gala Dali painted like an angel with wings, floating in the air about as high as a basketball net while below a quartet of men, one with a cockeyed grin, looked up under her dress. She was dressed in black—the real Gala, not the one in the painting. I figured her for thirty-five, her face pale and not quite pretty but clear, her dark hair brushed back. She was a woman who took the world seriously, which was probably quite a problem, since not many people in the world were prepared to take her husband seriously.

"Dali will be down in a minute," she said. "He just awakened from his dreams and is dressing. Please sit."

I sat in a wooden chair painted black.

"I'll be out working on the Hup if you need me," Zeman said to both Gala and me. Though it was his house, the information didn't seem to be of much interest to her. She looked at me with dark, dark eyes, trying to see something that would tell if I was worthy of an audience with the great man.

Zeman went back outside and Gala was alone with me, her hands clasped together in front of her like a concerned Mexican chaperone.

"The clocks," she said. "I want the clocks returned, but Dali's paintings are more important."

"What do they look like? The clocks and the paintings?"

"Only Dali can truly describe his own work," she said with pride. "The clocks are for the table, the size of two heads high and numbers in gold. They are deep, dark red-stained birch wood from the Ural mountains and on the bottom of each clock is an inscription in Russian. How did you break your nose?"

"It says, 'How did you break your nose' in Russian?"

"You are trying to be witty," she said dryly.

"My brother broke my nose, twice," I said.

"He wanted to break your nose?"

"The second time, probably. First time was an accident. He was a violent kid. He's a violent man."

"Brothers are serpents of the mind." The voice came from the stairway on my left.

I looked up. Dali stood at the top of the stairs dressed in a clown's outfit, a big floppy red suit with puffy white buttons, oversized slap-shoes. He wore no makeup. He didn't need any. I watched him come down the stairs and enter.

It wasn't a bad entrance as entrances go, but I've lived in and around Hollywood for almost half a century and I'd served security stints when I was with Warner Brothers and on my own. My favorite was the night Thelma Todd walked into a Victor McLaglin party, took off her white mink coat, and revealed one hell of a beautiful nude body. She looked down as if her having nothing on was a complete surprise. I was at the door, backing up the butler to keep out crashers. I saw Thelma Todd from behind. Dali in a clown suit didn't come close.

Dali came in, looked at his wife—who nodded—and examined me, touching his nose from time to time as if he were considering how to put me into one of his paintings. I didn't like the idea.

"Brothers are vampires," he said. "Brothers are vampires and fathers are ghouls. Mothers are saints whom we mistreat. You agree?"

He stopped circling and waited for my answer. Gala seemed to draw in her breath. Somewhere outside and not too far away a noisy lawn mower was being pushed.

"No," I said.

"You need money?" he asked, pointing his chin at me. "You want to work?"

"It's either that or learn to barter," I said. "And I've got nothing to trade with."

"I like you, Peters," he said with an accent that couldn't decide whether it was French or Spanish. "You have the face of a peasant."

"Thank you," I said.

"But I have liked Fascists and Surrealists," he whispered, leaning toward me so the Fascists and Surrealists would not hear him. "The Fascists wear brown shirts that look like the *merde* and the Surrealists paint with the *merde*. They have much in common."

"Then I withdraw my thanks."

"You think Dali is mad?" he asked, now moving to the matching white chair across from me and trying to sit in it with back-erect dignity, which is hard to do when you're wearing an oversized red suit and size 30 shoes. Gala moved forward to stand behind him and put her hands on both his shoulders. He reached up with both hands and touched hers. It looked like genuine affection, but I wasn't the one to recognize genuine affection.

"I don't know," I answered.

"The difference between me—" he pointed to himself in a grand gesture—"and a madman is that I am not mad."

He had said that before. I knew it, but instead of pointing it out I took a chance and said, "Are we going to keep it up like this or is there some place on the program when we have an intermission and you tell me what I'm doing here?"

"He is rude, Dali," Gala said, lifting her chin imperiously.

Dali patted her hands to reassure her.

"Dali is rude," he said. "He is honest. Would you like something to drink, Toby Peters?"

"Pepsi if you've got it. RC will do. Water with ice, if it comes to that."

Gala left the room. I thought she was going for my drink. She never came back with it.

When she was gone, Dali turned to me.

"Three things I wish to tell you," he said, holding up his right hand in a closed fist. "First"—and one finger came up—"I love American radio but your announcers, actors speak too fast. Second"—second finger—"I must have my paintings back, and Gala's clocks."

His left hand went into the pocket of his clown suit

and came out with an oddly shaped piece of wood. He played with the wood while we kept talking.

"What were they paintings of and how big are they?" I asked.

"One was the size of that one," he said, pointing at a painting about the size of the front of a refrigerator. "Another was the size of that wall."

"Big picture," I said.

"Magnificent picture," he agreed. "Months to paint."

"Third picture," I said.

His face went slack, the bug-eyed Huntz Hall look disappeared. The mask dropped and he looked human, frightened.

"It is like this," he said, standing and holding his arms out to show me that the missing painting was about a yard across and a yard and a half high.

"They'll be hard to find if I don't know what they look like," I prodded.

"They are unmistakably Dali's," he said, a touch of the normal still there. "And that is the problem."

"I'm not an art critic or an artist," I said.

"And I am not a detective," he said.

I spent the next half hour asking him questions while he fidgeted with the piece of wood and paced around the room. The paintings and the clocks had been taken from his house in Carmel about a month ago. It had happened during the night when he and his wife were asleep. All of the paintings had been framed; they had been taken frame and all.

"What can they do with these paintings?"

"Probably nothing while Dali lives," he said. "Nothing but show them to or sell them to people who will appreciate them. When Dali dies, they will be worth much and these . . . these insects can claim Dali sold the paintings to them or gave them."

"So you're afraid they might kill you so they can sell them and kick the price up?"

The reaction made it clear that Dali had never considered that possibility. He stopped pacing and looked at me. He blinked like an owl, his mouth opened. He froze.

"You think they . . . ?"

"No," I said. "Not a chance. These are art thieves, not people willing to risk a murder charge for a few thousand dollars."

"Many thousand dollars," Dali corrected.

"Many thousand dollars," I agreed.

"Your wife says you got a note. Can I see it?"

Dali plunged his hand into the clown pocket and came up with a crumpled envelope. He handed it to me and stood back to watch my reaction. I pulled a sheet of paper out of the envelope. The words were typed and there weren't many of them:

> *Look for the second PLACE in Los Angeles to find the first painting. You have till midnight on New Year's Day.*

I looked up at Dali.

"You may keep it," he said.

I nodded sagely.

"You know what it means, these words?" he asked.

"Do you?" I asked right back with a knowing smile as I stood and pocketed the envelope and letter.

"No," he said. "But there is only one reason this *ladron* would send such a note. He wishes to toy with Dali, to drive Dali mad, but Dali is beyond madness. *Madness* is a word without meaning."

I asked some more questions but didn't get very much that would help. He had no idea who would steal his paintings. It wasn't that he didn't suspect anyone. He started on a list of those he did not trust. I wrote the names but gave up after twenty when he began to include people from his childhood, some of whom were dead. The list included Pablo Picasso, Luis Bunuel, Andre Breton, Dali's father, and Francisco Franco.

"Zeman," I tried.

"Yes, I do not trust him," Dali said emphatically. "I trust only Gala. I do not even trust Dali. He is totally unreliable."

"I'll bear that in mind," I said. "One hundred dollars in advance and I'll call you every day." I moved toward the door and Dali followed, his clown feet plopping on the hardwood floor.

"Gala gave me the money," he said, pulling out a handful of bills and handing them to me. He put his hand back in his pocket and came out with more. I stopped at the door and counted while he played with his mustache and looked at a blank wall. He was two bucks short but what the hell.

"You'll hear from me," I said.

"You must find those paintings," Dali whispered. "I've painted what I see within me, without censorship. The world knows that Dali fears no offense, but this painting . . . it will end the career of Salvador Dali. Find them all, but find that one and Dali owes you his art."

He took my hand in both of his after pocketing the piece of wood he had been playing with.

"I'll settle for twenty a day, expenses, and that painting," I said, opening the door. "One more thing."

"One more thing," Dali repeated.

"When we started talking, you said you had three things to tell me. You only told me two of them."

Dali smiled as I stepped outside.

"The third thing is that no one knows who I really am. On Tuesday there is a party in Carmel. On Tuesday, I will be both a rabbit and Sherlock Holmes."

With that, he closed the door.

Zeman was working under the hood of the Hup. He stopped and moved over to my car as I crawled over the passenger side to the driver's seat. There was no way to do it gracefully. I rolled down the window to hear what he had to say.

"How'd it go?" he asked.

"Not much to go on," I said.

"How'd you like them?" He nodded toward his own front door as if they might come out for a curtain call. I shrugged.

"I can see where they might be a little tough to come home to every night."

"Make it a thousand-dollar bonus if you find them in three days, Peters," he said as I turned the key and prayed for the Crosley to start. It didn't. I was left filled with incentive and no idea of what the hell to do to find the missing paintings.

"What about the clocks?" I asked.

"Good pieces," he said. "Might be worth a few thousand each. More if they work."

"They don't work?"

"No one has ever wound them," he said. "Gala says they were gifts to the Russian royal family, but the tsar never got to use them. Revolution came before they could be wound . . . or something. She and her family got them out and haven't allowed anyone to wind them."

"Why would anyone take clocks and paintings and then write crazy messages?" I asked.

"I'm an investor, not a detective," Zeman said with a shrug as he moved away from the door. "Ask me about Dusenbergs or Brazilian bonds."

I started the engine, heard it ping to life. I put it in gear as the front door to Zeman's house opened and Gala Dali stepped out holding a glass of bubbling dark liquid.

My Pepsi. I put the car into gear and headed for what passed for sanity in Los Angeles.

It was about seven when I hit Main Street looking for a place to buy a Pepsi and get a sandwich. Not much was open on New Year's Day, not even Manny's taco stand on Hoover. Usually I left the car at No-Neck Arnie's, but everything was closed and there were plenty of parking spaces, including one right in front of the Farraday.

The streets weren't deserted. They hadn't been deserted in downtown Los Angeles since the war had started. Nightfall and the blackout did put a damper on the town but didn't close it down—it just went undercover. The outer door to the Farraday was open but the one inside was locked. Jeremy Butler had started locking it when even he was forced to acknowledge that he was losing the battle against bums looking for a corner of cool tile. It wasn't actually a battle; Jeremy never complained about the bums. He never complained about anything. He went about his business, Lysol in great hairy hand and a poem forming in the mind under the bullet-smooth cranium.

I listened to my footsteps echo across the inner lobby. There were a few lights on, enough to find your way to the stairs and elevator, but not enough to penetrate the far corners.

The Farraday was silent and I was in no hurry. I had about five hours till midnight and a puzzle to work on. I didn't think I'd solve it. I took the elevator, an ornate wire cage from the days of Diamond Jim Brady. The elevator never quite came awake. It moved slowly upward in a swaying daze. Usually I walked.

On the way up I looked through the chipped gilt mesh at the offices on each floor where lies were sold. You want a lie to believe in? The Farraday was the place for it. Want to become a movie star? There were four agents in the Farraday. Want to sue everyone who ever told you the truth about yourself? You had a choice of lawyers, almost one to every floor. Did you want to think you were irresistible? Escort services for ladies and gents were on the second and fifth floor. Want to think you're beautiful? Choice of two photographers, one of which was Maurice, Photographer to the Stars. The other was Josh Copeland, Glamour Portraits at a Reasonable Price. Bookies, pornographers, doctors of everything from throat to stomach, a single dentist—Sheldon Minck— who sold the promise of a winning smile and perpetual Sen-Sen breath. And then there was me on the sixth floor, where the elevator came to a jerky stop. I sold the lie that there was always one last chance when all reasonable attempts to solve your problems failed. Sometimes, usually because it was easy or I was lucky, I actually helped a client.

I pushed open the hinged metal doors and heard their clang echo down the halls and into the lobby below. I took a step toward the "suite" I shared with Sheldon Minck, D.D.S., S.D. (The S.D. was Shelly's invention. It meant either "Special Dentist" or "Superb Dentures" or whatever he thought up that week.)

Someone laughed behind a door on the floor above. I recognized the laughter—it had come from Alice Pallis, wife of Jeremy Butler, mother of Natasha Butler. When Alice laughed it did more than echo. When Alice cried, it did more than moan. Alice was massive, almost as big as Jeremy. She had once had an office in the Farraday in which she published pornography. Jeremy had made her see the light and together they produced a baby and little books of poetry. They lived in the Farraday. They were the only ones who did, or wanted to.

I took out my key and went into the reception room of the office. I hit the light switch and didn't bother to look around. The reception room was about the size of the inside of a Frigidaire. It smelled like an ashtray and was strewn with magazines, on the floor, the little table, and both of the mismatched waiting chairs. I picked up a three-month-old *Life* magazine and opened the inner door.

Shelly's office offered a richer panorama of smells: a combination of wintergreen, cloves, cigars, stale food, and days-old coffee. It smelled like that for a good reason. I found the light switch on the wall, hit it, and discovered Dr. Sheldon Minck himself, asleep in his dental chair and fully dressed in gray trousers, a plaid jacket, a white shirt, and a tie that looked like the tongue of a giraffe I liked to feed in the Griffith Park Zoo. Shelly's pudgy hands were clasped in front of him on his stomach, rising and falling with each overweight exhalation of air. A little pointed cardboard party hat was perched on his bald head. The rubber band intended to keep it there had crept up to his nose in an attempt to meet the thick glasses, which were creeping downward. Clamped in the right corner of his mouth was an unlit and particularly rancid-looking cigar.

I found myself wishing Dali were there to see the sight. I considered turning and getting the hell out of there before I had to deal with whatever had brought Shelly here on New Year's Day. Instead of leaving, I tiptoed to the broom closet I used for an office, opened the door—taking about a month to do it so it wouldn't wake Shelly—and went in. It was almost dark outside now but I didn't turn on the light. I went behind my desk, opened the window behind it that looked down on an alley, and sat down, placing the *Life* magazine and the letter to Dali in front of me in an area of the desk relatively free of bills and old newspapers.

I looked around the room in the orange twilight and saw what I always see, two chairs squeezed in on the other side of the desk, and a wall with my Private Investigator's license and a photograph—a photograph of me, my brother Phil, my father, and our dog, Kaiser Wilhelm. I was ten in that picture. Phil was fifteen. My mother was dead. My father soon would be. No one knows what happened to Kaiser Wilhelm. He just had enough one day and wandered off, some say in the direction of Alaska.

I wasn't sure of the time. My old man's watch didn't help. It promised me it was two-thirty and that for sure was a lie, but I forgave it. I could have turned on the little white Arvin on my desk, a birthday gift a month ago from Gunther Wherthman. It was almost time for the Rex Stout show, but I didn't want to wake Shelly beyond the door. I should have been thinking about Dali's stolen paintings. I tried, but I found myself wondering what Gwen and Gunther looked like in mad embrace. I got no picture so I picked up the *Life* and squinted at it, holding it up so the last of the sun would hit the pages. I learned a lot about Admiral Leahy, a little about aerial navigation, and too much about why the Yankees won the American League championship. Then the sun was gone and I had to turn the light on.

I got up, moved slowly to the switch near the door, and watched the overhead 100-watt Mazda in a round white-glass globe go into action. I'd lost about an hour. I scratched the fingers of my left hand with the fingers of my right and went back to the desk.

Look for the second PLACE in Los Angeles to find the first painting. You have till midnight on New Year's Day.

I pulled out my spiral pocket notebook and opened it to the page where I'd written the names of Dali's suspects. Maybe I should start with Picasso? I needed Dash. He could distract me. Maybe I should sail paper airplanes out the window?

I was considering these options when the door to my office opened and Shelly walked in, a rolled-up dental journal in his hand. I could tell it was a dental journal by the smiling incisor on the curved cover.

"I thought you were a burglar," he said, lowering the weapon.

"And you were going to beat the hell out of him with the *Dental Times?*"

"*Dental Hygiene,*" he corrected.

He still wore the little hat but the rubber band was back under one of his chins where it belonged. The cigar was in his hand and his glasses were pushed back on his nose. He plopped heavily into one of the chairs in front of the desk.

"Phones keep going out," he said. "Tried to call Mildred a few minutes ago."

"That's nice, Shel," I said.

"To be expected," said Shel. "Got a patient—Leon, you know? Big guy with lots of ear hair."

"I'm working, Shel," I said.

"Leon says more than forty-three thousand Bell employees are in the armed services. He says there are copper shortages. Lucky to have phones at all, Leon says. You want to hear what happened to me?"

"No," I said.

"Someone made a pass at Mildred again. You know who?"

"Sydney Greenstreet."

"No, no. Murray Taibo's brother, Simon, the accountant," Shelly said, shaking his head in exasperation. "You know Mildred is irresistible."

I said nothing. Mildred is a rake with a prune attached where a head should be. Mildred had, about a year ago, kicked Shelly out and run off with a Peter Lorre imitator. When the guy had been killed, Mildred went back to Shelly.

"I know," I said.

"We had words, you know?"

"I can guess."

"I was a little drunk," said Shelly, looking at the palm of his left hand as if it had the answer to a question he was about to ask. "I said things. I was crazed, Toby, crazed. There is just so much a man can take, even if he is a board-certified dentist."

What is there to say in the face of such wisdom?

"Anyway," he said, "I think I told Mildred I was not coming home. So, here I am."

"Here you are," I agreed.

We sat in silence for about a minute and then he remarked, "It was a nice party."

"I'm sure. Who would expect less from Murray Taibo?"

"Right."

"I've got work to do, Shel," I said, looking down at the thief's note. "And time's running out."

"You want something to eat? I brought stuff from the party."

"Let's take a look."

He went out, leaving the door open, and returned in a few seconds with a grease-stained brown paper bag which he placed on the desk in front of me. I opened it and fished out a quartet of hors d'oeuvres on little slices of stale white bread shaped like hearts, clubs, diamonds, and spades. The stuff on them was creamy, orange, and sad. There was also a slice of chocolate cake. I ate a busted flush and the cake while Shelly, having paid for the time with leftovers, went on about the beauty of Mildred and the pangs of jealousy.

"You want to help?" I interrupted. "Take your mind off your troubles?"

"Why not?" He shrugged.

"Take off the hat," I said.

He took off the hat and put it on the corner of my desk. I gave him a shorthand version of the little I knew about the Dali theft.

"Now look at this," I said, handing him the note.

He held his glasses to keep them from falling and squinted at the note. The writing was large and clear. He handed the sheet back to me.

"Well?" I said.

"You've only got three hours," Shelly answered, looking at his watch. "I've been gone almost two nights. I think I'll go home." He got up and headed for the door.

"Thanks, Shel," I said, dropping crumbs into the now empty brown bag.

"Dali's the painter who does the crazy stuff, right?" asked Shelly, turning toward me with an idea.

I nodded.

"You think you could talk him into painting a big tooth for me? You know, a tooth with a smile?"

"No, Shelly."

"How do you know? You haven't asked him."

"I know."

Shelly, unconvinced, retrieved his hat and went out, leaving the door open behind him. I looked at the note a few thousand times more and wondered what *the second place* in Los Angeles was. I wasn't even sure what the first place was—the Brown Derby, Paramount, M.G.M.? I knew it wasn't Columbia or Warners. Sunset or Hollywood Boulevard? The Beverly Hills Hotel? A little after ten and hungry again, I stuffed the note in my pocket, closed the window, turned out the light, and left the suites of Minck and Peters.

I was on the way down the stairs when I heard something move in the sixth-floor shadows. I stopped and waited a beat. Jeremy Butler stepped out.

"This is not a day of work," he said. He was wearing dark trousers and a black turtleneck shirt. He had put on a few pounds in the ten years since he had stopped wrestling, but the arms and shoulders were still solid as a telephone pole.

"I've got a deadline," I said.

"If we do not accept the events that mark the mythical passage of the year, if we do not honor the rituals and landmarks of time, great and small, seasonal and personal, we demean existence and its meaning. We demean ourselves."

I didn't know what the hell he was talking about, but shook my head and smiled as if I did.

"What are you working on?"

I told him quickly and he listened quietly.

"Salvador Dali is a tormented man," he said when I finished. "When one lives the lie of madness long enough, one inevitably becomes mad and it is no longer a lie. One is trapped within the illusion that he can remove the mask, but he dare not try for fear that he will be unable to do it. The tragedy of Salvador Dali is that he thinks he is a clown claiming to be a genius when in fact he is a genius who truly believes himself to be only a clown."

"How did you figure all this out, Jeremy?"

"From his paintings, his autobiography. It was published last year, a sad attempt to shock."

"What do you make of this?" I said, handing him the note.

He held it up to the light from the yellow bulb on the sixth-floor landing and read, then he returned the note to me.

"The word PLACE is capitalized," he said.

"I noticed."

"It may be a proper name," he said.

"The second Place?"

"The second person named Place in Los Angeles," he said.

"What second person named Place?"

"Perhaps," he said, "the second person named Place in the Los Angeles telephone directory."

4

Jeremy went back to his family and I went for the phone book in my office, hoping the right pages hadn't been torn out by Dash during one of his visits. The page was there. The first Place listed was Aaron. He was followed by Adam Place, who lived on Nicholas in Culver City. It was a little after eleven. I considered calling but what would I say? "Have you got a stolen Dali painting?"

About twenty minutes later I was pulling into a parking spot on Nicholas across from Lindberg Park. There was no one on the street when I crawled out of the passenger seat of my Crosley and looked around for the address. It wasn't hard to find, a rectangular one-story pink adobe house across the street in the middle of a block. There was a white sign in front of the house announcing ADAM PLACE, TAXIDERMY.

From what I could see, Adam was asleep or out. No hint of light seeped through or around the closed vertical blinds covering every window. I went up the little walkway, stopped, and listened. I couldn't hear any-thing. There was a white button next to the door. I pushed it, but didn't hear any gong, buzz, bell, or clang. I tried again. Nothing. I knocked. The knock echoed down the block and into the rustling trees across the street in Lindberg Park. I knocked again.

Then I tried the door. Locked. It must have been near twelve and I had to make up my mind. Knocking was getting me nowhere. I could get back in my Crosley, watch the place and wait for a light or a human or the morning. That would definitely put me past the midnight deadline the thief had given. I stepped off the path and moved around to the side of the house. No point in trying a front window and risk being seen. The houses on either side of the adobe were barricaded by bushes. I went to the left and looked for a window and shadows to hide in. I found both. The first win-dow was locked but the second one was open. I shoved it, pushed the blinds out of the way, and climbed in. When I got inside, I turned and closed the window behind me.

Darkness and the overwhelming smell of something dry and old. I followed the wall to the right, hand over hand, feeling for a light switch or a lamp. Adam Place, if he had a gun and was somewhere in here, had a perfect right to blow my head off. I thought about that as I moved along, figuring I'd eventually hit the front door and find some kind of light. It didn't take that long. I bumped into furniture, tripped over a table, felt some-thing brush my face and fall behind me, and then I felt it. Definitely a lamp. I turned it on and found myself looking into the angry face and sharp teeth of an animal about the size of my Crosley. I stepped backward, fell over a table full of stuffed birds, and landed on the floor in a flurry of dead wings. The animal with the angry face and sharp teeth was a puma. I'd seen one in the Griffith Park Zoo. This one was stuffed and dead.

If Adam Place was here, I was a noisy dead man, but no one came running or calling. I sat up, brushed away owls, gulls, doves, and a small eagle, and looked around the room. The lamp cast a washed-out yellowish circle of light over a room cluttered with stuffed animals looking directly at me. There were dozens of them, covering almost every spot of table, mantle, shelf, and even floor. And on the walls were paintings of animals. The wall was covered with paintings of elephants, bears, lions, the big ones looking just as stuffed as the ones below them. I got up and looked around, being careful where I stepped.

Through doves, squirrels, raccoons, rabbits, and even a pair of armadillos, I tiptoed my way across the room to the next room. There was a light switch in there, just inside the doorway. I hit it and looked around what must once have been a dining room. Now it was just an extension off the living room. More paintings on the wall. Stuffed animals, some as small as mice, covered the chairs and filled a huge china cabinet whose doors were open. The big wooden table with claw feet was crowded with animals in various states of stuffing. A possum, its belly open and half filled with sawdust, lay on its back surrounded by sharp metal instruments.

I wanted to whistle "Violets for Your Furs" and go for the door, but I backed out of the room and went on. The house was small. There couldn't have been much left. Somewhere in the darkness I could hear the serious ticking of a clock. I went through a kitchen, which had not yet been completely overtaken by dead animals but was well on the way, and found a bathroom. I hit the light and saw a sink, tub, wicker clothes hamper, and one stuffed animal, a small alligator, perched on the toilet bowl.

I moved back into the hall and found the first bed-room, or what should have been the bedroom but was the reptile room. Tables of snakes, lizards, and things I didn't want to look at too closely. One wall was free of paintings. It was filled by a floor-to-ceiling bookcase. All the books were, I was sure, about animals and how to do them in or do them up.

I figured it for a two-bedroom house and I was right. I found the switch in the second one and saw a stuffed grizzly bear in the middle of the room, guarding a big bed on which a man lay in roughly the same position as the possum in the dining room. There was a black, bloody hole in his forehead and a surprised look on his face. At the foot of the bed on a little table sat a big clock, Gala Dali's clock, ticking, its face toward the dead man, now beyond time. The bed, neatly made, was covered in blood.

Over the bed on the wall was a painting. Dali was right. It was unmistakably his. It wasn't very big and nothing like the other paintings in the house, except that the biggest figure was clearly an animal, a big white bird with a long neck and the head of a man wearing a derby hat. The bird was full of holes you could see through to a ridge of rocks behind it in sand. The Swiss cheese bird didn't seem to be uncomfortable.

The bird wasn't easy to make out because someone had used white paint to splash across the picture the words:

> *Señor, 13th Street at midnight tomorrow in the Town of the Spectator.*

I checked the time on Gala's clock. It was ten after midnight. Tomorrow had already started. I moved to the bed and pushed the dead guy over just enough to reach into his pocket and pull out his wallet with the not-too-

clean handkerchief I had in my pocket. I didn't get much
blood on the handkerchief.

The dead guy was Adam Place, or someone carrying
Place's wallet. There were two tens and a single in the
wallet, plus some pictures of the dead guy in an army
uniform—World War I, not the current one. I dropped
the wallet and moved to the phone near the clock. I got
a cop on duty at the Wilshire Station and with my best
Polish-Hungarian-Czech accent said, "Is man dead
here."

"How should I know?" asked the cop.

"No," I said. "Is here, here a man dead in his bed. Very
blood. Very dead. You come."

"Where?" asked the cop, without enthusiasm.

I gave him the address.

"Wait there," he said.

I hung up and looked up at the painting. It wouldn't do
Dali much good and it was evidence, an oversized piece
of evidence. But he was my client and the only thing I
had to sell was loyalty.

"What the hell," I said to the grizzly bear, and leaned
over the bed to get the painting down. I considered
taking the clock, too, but I couldn't carry the painting,
the handkerchief I needed to wipe away my prints, and
the clock, which looked as if it weighed about as much as
Shelly Minck's dental chair. If I hurried, I could get the
painting in the car and come back for the clock.

With the painting under my arm I made my way out of
the bedroom, turning off the light behind me. I hit the
other lights and went to the front door. I had at least ten
minutes to get out of the area, maybe more. The cop on
duty hadn't believed me but he'd follow through and a
patrol would amble over and check it out about the time
I was pulling up in front of Mrs. Plaut's too late to get
Apples Eisenhower.

I was wrong. I turned the latch with my handkerchiefed hand, opened the door carefully, and found myself looking at two uniformed policemen. The bigger one had his hand up ready to knock.

What was there to say? I pocketed the bloody handkerchief and said, "Yes, officers?"

"Got a problem here, sir?"

"Problem?" I said.

"Neighbor said there were noises, lights, saw someone crawling through a window," said the smaller cop, who looked a little like Jimmy Cagney.

Both of them had their hands on their holsters. I kept mine in front of me.

"Noises?" I asked.

"Noises," said Jimmy Cagney.

"And a man crawling in a window," said the bigger guy.

"Where were you going with that painting, sir?" asked Cagney.

"Going?" I said, brilliantly.

"And what did you put in your pocket?" said the big guy, holding out his hand.

"I . . ."

"Just take it out slowly," said Cagney, pulling his pistol and aiming it at my chest.

I pulled out the bloody handkerchief and offered it to the big cop. There wasn't much light, but it was enough for them to see the blood.

"I think we're coming in," said Cagney.

"I think you are," I agreed, stepping back.

It moved fast from that point. I was in handcuffs and on my way to the station in five minutes. I knew what the charge would be. Neither of the cops had bothered to ask me questions. Why should they? They had called in for the medical examiner and a homicide crew and we were on the way down the street with the painting in the trunk when a second patrol car pulled around the corner. We didn't stop. I figured the second car was coming in answer to my call. They'd go in and find the body, too. It would probably take the L.A.P.D. a week to figure out what had happened.

No one talked to me that night. I asked to see my brother but no one paid attention. I wasn't sure whether they believed Phil was my brother or they just didn't care. I was in the Culver City lockup, and he was sleeping in North Hollywood. They took my ninety-eight dollars. I got a receipt.

The cop who took my prints was about seventy. He said they'd picked up a guy the week before because of his prints.

"Robbed a guy and beat him near bloody death," the old cop said. "But the victim bit one of the assailant's fingers off. Took a print from the bit-off finger and tracked him in a week."

"Life's little ironies," I said.

"Ain't that the truth," said the old cop.

I had a cell to myself. They do that with people suspected of being homicidal maniacs. It saves the embarrassment of explaining the violent overnight deaths of other prisoners.

All in all it had been one lousy day. I was sure I'd be up looking for dawn through the barred window and listening to other prisoners snore. I lay on the cot, put my head on my rolled-up windbreaker, and was asleep before I could remember what had been written on the Dali painting.

I dreamed of birds flying over a desert. The birds had vacant looks and their feet were stuck to little pedestals. They were searching for something, blocking out the sun, and Dali was there, in front of a giant nude woman sitting with her back to me. The woman was looking at one of Gala's clocks, the one I had seen in Place's bedroom. The clock was melting. Dali was wearing his big red suit and slap-shoes. Behind him was Koko the Clown, who flapped his arms and flew up in the sky with the birds. Dali danced over to me, a paintbrush in his hand, and dabbed a smear of white on my nose. I couldn't move my arms.

He leaned over and whispered to me as Koko swooped down and stuck out his tongue.

"Listen to me. There is no longer a second place, and there is no Thirteenth Street in the present tense. Time is death."

I wanted to shoo him away but my hands wouldn't move. I didn't want any more puzzles or riddles. My head throbbed from the sound of dead birds, and I longed for a simple missing senile grandmother, a play-around husband, or a murder for ten bucks by a dim-witted armed robber. My wishes were simple even in my dreams.

Dali danced off and Koko landed in front of me. The birds filled the sky, blotting out the sun, and Koko opened his mouth to tell me the answer to the puzzle.

"Get up," he said.

That wasn't the answer and it wasn't Koko's voice. I opened my eyes and looked into the face of a uniformed cop with a freckled bald head. The sun was coming in through the bars, and I could smell something that might be food.

"Up, Peters," the cop said.

I sat up.

"No clowns," I said.

"Just you, bub," the cop said wearily. "They want you upstairs. Got your legs?"

"Yeah."

"Let's go," said the cop and we went.

Up two flights of stairs and two minutes later with the cop behind me I saw my face in the mirror of a candy machine. The stubble was almost a beard and it was gray.

"That door," he said. "Left."

I went through the door and found myself in an interrogation room: one table, four chairs, one lieutenant I knew named Seidman, and my brother, Phil. Lieutenant Steve Seidman, tall, thin, and white-faced, not because he was a mime but because he hated the sun, leaned back against the wall, holding his hat in his hand. He didn't have much hair left, but that didn't stop him from patting it down and giving me a shake of the head that said, *Toby, Toby, this time you've really done it.*

My brother, Captain Phil Pevsner, was not shaking his head. He sat in a chair behind the desk, hands palm down on a green ink-stained blotter, eyes looking through me.

Phil was a little taller than me, broader, older, with close-cut steely hair and a hard cop's gut. His tie always dangled loosely around his neck, as it did now, and his face often turned red with contained rage, especially when I was in the same room . . . or even on the same planet. Today's tie was a dark, solid blue; standard Phil.

For some reason, "How are Ruth and the kids?" were the magic words that usually brought Phil out of a chair, a corner, or a daydream and into my face and lungs. He had decided years ago that I asked him about his family just to provoke him. He had been wrong the first three times.

"Happy New Year," I said cheerfully.

Phil came around the desk like a bear with a mission. I knew I had found three new words to drive him mad. Seidman moved quickly from the wall and got between me and my brother. Seidman was a pro with more than seven years experience of saving me from Phil Pevsner brutality.

"Phil," Seidman said, making it sound like my brother should remember something about his own name.

"Move, Steve," Phil said, looking past his partner and into my smiling face.

"Phil," Seidman repeated, holding his hands up but not touching my brother. Even he was not ready for that.

"He's laughing at me," Phil said. "Does he know what kind of shit he's in this time?"

"He's got a lot on his mind," said Seidman.

"He's right," I said sincerely.

"Shit," said my brother, holding up his hands to show his palms to Seidman and to me. He backed up, went around the desk, and sat heavily. The chair made a rusty squeal as he turned away and found a fascinating squashed beetle to look at on the wall. I had the rush of an idea that Phil and Dali might have a lot in common. I hoped they would never have the chance for a discussion of contemporary art. It would either end with Dali dead or Phil in a straight-jacket.

"Sit down, Toby," Seidman said, moving back to the wall and patting down his wisps of hair.

I sat down in the chair across from Phil.

The war had been Phil's big break. He had been promoted right up the ladder from Homicide Sergeant to Detective Captain of the whole Wilshire District. Seidman had moved up with him. The rise hadn't been because of Phil's skills, but in spite of them. Phil was a basher. Phil hated criminals, sincerely hated them. Phil wanted to end all crime but knew it would never happen. The resulting frustration meant that every time he came face-to-face with a felon he became enraged. Other cops loved Phil. He was the one you frightened suspects with. No one in homicide had to play bad cop. They just called Phil or, if the criminal had been around a while, they just evoked his name. But the armed forces had taken the younger, ambitious police talent and Phil had been promoted to a job he hated, sitting behind a desk dealing with complaints from vendors about cops taking avocados, filling out forms, talking to visiting Chambers of Commerce from Quincy, Illinois. He had lasted about a year as boss of the Wilshire and then had been booted back to homicide after too many complaints. Seidman had asked to go back to homicide with him. Phil had been happy with the demotion. His wife, Ruth, with three kids in the house, had resumed worrying about her husband's high blood pressure.

"I appreciate your coming," I said.

Seidman shook his head; Phil said nothing and kept staring at the bug.

"Did you kill him?" asked Seidman.

"No, Steve. Am I a killer?"

"Toby, don't answer my questions with questions. Phil and I leave and two guys who don't know you are going to come through that door and put you on the top of page two of the *Times*."

"I didn't kill him," I said.

"Ask him about the handkerchief," said Phil, very softly.

"You had a bloody handkerchief," said Seidman, who was back to playing with his hat.

What could I say? It was bloody because I used it to fish Adam Place's wallet out of his pocket and put it back and then wipe my fingerprints off the doorknobs?

"I didn't do it, Phil," I said to my brother's back.

"Ask him about breaking in," said Phil.

"Did you—" Seidman began, but I jumped in.

"Can we eliminate the middleman here? Maybe we can save a little time and you can find the killer."

"If I talk to him, I kill him," said Phil. "He's made my life a toilet." Phil leaned forward and punched the wall about two inches above the bug, leaving a depression in the general shape and size of a fist.

"I can deal with a middleman," I said. "I went into Place's house because I was on a job. I had reason to believe a valuable piece of property had been taken by Place and would be destroyed by midnight. I knocked at the door. He didn't answer. I went in through the window, found him, and called the police immediately."

"You pick up a Hunky accent during the night?" said Phil, forgetting immediately that we had agreed on a middleman.

"I didn't want to get involved."

"What about the painting?" asked Seidman.

"My client's. It was stolen."

"It was a mess," said Seidman.

"I was going to give it back anyway," I said. "You got me for picking up stolen property and trying to return it. By the way, the clock in Place's bedroom—that was my client's, too."

"We got you for breaking and entering, burglary, homicide, and attempting to leave the scene of a felony," said Seidman, ignoring my addition of the clock to the problem.

"I wasn't leaving. I was going outside to wait for the police."

"Were you going to talk to them in Bohemian?" asked Phil.

I didn't like it when I couldn't see his face. I didn't know if he was boiling up or cooling down.

"I made a mistake," I said.

"Maybe your client got there first, and when he saw what Place had done to the painting he went nuts and killed him," Seidman suggested.

"No, not this client," I said.

"Who is he?" Phil said, so softly I almost missed it.

Now I was scared. Just before Phil completely lost control he made one last effort, always a failure, to be so calm and quiet that the unwary might think he had dozed off. But I had almost half a century of experience.

"Come on," I said. "You know I can't tell you."

Phil spun around and looked at me. He was grinning. I had never seen that before.

"He's a suspect," Phil said. "And we're going to get him or you're going to go up on charges of interfering with a homicide investigation."

"What about murder?"

"Medical examiner says Place was shot before eight," said Seidman. "Both your landlord at the Farraday, Butler, and Minck say you were in the Farraday till eleven."

"The bullet, Steve," I said. "Is it from a thirty-eight? My gun's a thirty-eight and I haven't fired it. You can take it to ballistics."

Seidman shifted and looked uneasy.

"Can't match the bullet. No known make or caliber."

"Look for the second Place in Los Angeles to find the first painting. You have till midnight on New Year's Day," said Phil, looking directly at me with that new grin. "We found the note in your wallet. You were too late, Tobias."

"We're playing with a wacko," said Seidman. "Did this guy kill Place just because he had the second name in the phone book?"

"Which of you figured it out?" I asked, my eyes fixed on my brother's face for the slightest twitch that would tell me he was ready to attack, and that neither Seidman nor the Fifth Army would stop him.

"It didn't take much," Phil said. "We had a clue you didn't mention. Place's dead body."

"Look—" I started.

"No, you listen," Phil said. "You'll find the next on Thirteenth Street at midnight tomorrow."

"In the town of the spectator," I added.

"What?" asked Phil, sensing a needle.

"The writing on the painting. It ended with 'the Town of the Spectator,'" Seidman explained.

"Who gives a shit?" said Phil. "There is no Thirteenth Street in Los Angeles. There are only seven listings for Street in the phone book and there's no Thirteenth Street. Pico is Thirteenth Street. There's a Thirteenth Avenue."

"He says Street, he means Street," I said.

"How many paintings are there, Toby?" asked Seidman. "Are they all by Dali? Who's the guy who owns the paintings, the guy you're working for?"

I sat up a little and pulled at my underwear. I was fragrant from the night in the lockup, fragrant and hungry.

"Come on, Steve," I said, hoping it didn't sound like a whine. "If I give you the name of my client, I'm out of business. My reputation will be shot. It's what I've got to sell."

"You can sell apples on the street in front of Union Station," said Phil. "I'll buy a dozen."

"Phil, you're my brother, and I really love you, but you've got no sense of humor."

This time the fist came down on the desk. Everything on the blotter and beyond, the in-box, a few pencils, the photograph of somebody's wife, danced around. Phil went cold blank, a very bad sign. Seidman saw it and stepped away from the wall again, motioning for me to get up. I figured he planned to block his partner, not enough to do much good but enough to give me a start out the door. I wasn't sure where I'd go when and if I did make it beyond the Coke machine.

"Phil," Seidman warned.

I started to get up.

"Let him go," said Phil, folding his hands in front of him on the desk, his knuckles going white.

"What?" asked Seidman.

"Let him go," Phil repeated. "Go downstairs with him and tell Liebowitz to let him go. Tell him I said so."

"Mike Liebowitz isn't going to—" Seidman began.

"Mike Liebowitz owes me his job," said brother Phil. "If he gives you a hard time, tell him to remember the Pacific Electric case in '36."

"Steve," I said. "It's a trick to get you out of the room."

"No trick," said Phil with a laugh. "I'm not in the mood for tricks."

He turned the squeaky swivel chair so he was facing the wall, and Seidman and I exchanged what's-going-on looks. Seidman shrugged first. Then he went out the door. Silence. The room needed a window.

"Phil," I said.

"Ruth's got a growth in her left breast," he said. "The doctor says it doesn't look good."

"Shit, Phil, I'm—"

"Just shut up, Toby," he cut in, holding his hammy right hand up.

I shut up. More silence.

"She needs surgery," he said. "Day after tomorrow. The boys don't know. Surgeons are fucking butchers. You know that?"

"Some of them—"

"They're butchers," he repeated.

"I play handball with a surgeon," I said. "Good one named Hodgdon. He's kind of old, specializes in bones, but he'd know a—"

Phil shook his head.

"Found out Wednesday," he said. "Hell of a New Year's present. We haven't told anybody, not even Ruth's mother."

"I'm sorry, Phil," I said.

"Yeah," he said. "Give her a call. Don't let her know you know."

"I will," I said. "Can I have Doc Hodgdon give you a call?"

Phil shrugged. "Ruth's got great teeth," he said. "The kids all have her teeth."

"Wouldn't be so bad if they had our teeth," I said.

"You know how old mom was when she died?" he asked.

"Forty-three," I said. I wasn't likely to forget. She died giving birth to me, which, I was sure, was one of the reasons Phil had decided before he even saw me that he would make my life miserable.

"Ruth is forty-three," he said.

"Come on, Phil. It's . . ."

The opening door stopped me.

Seidman. He looked at me and then at Phil's back and then back at me. I shrugged.

"You can walk," he said to me, and then to Phil, "Liebowitz says he's doing the papers and wants you to sign off. He says you answer to the D.A."

Phil laughed. It didn't seem very important to him. I got up and moved to the door.

"I'll call Ruth," I said.

"Thirteenth Street, Town of the Spectator," Phil answered. "You got till midnight."

There should have been more, but there wasn't. Phil didn't want more and I didn't know how to give it.

I moved past Seidman, went down the hall past the Coke machine and down the stairs to the desk to pick up my things. I signed for everything and got it all back except for the note to Dali. I didn't complain.

I took a cab back to Lindberg Park, paid with Dali's advance and made a note of the payment and tip as an expense item in my notebook. Across the street a cop was standing at the door to Place's place. He looked at me suspiciously. My khaki Crosley had been sitting there all night and was hard to miss. I got in the passenger side of the Crosley, which I had not locked the night before, and slid into the driver's seat. I was halfway down the block before the cop got into the street. In the rear-view mirror, I could see him writing my license number. I hope he got a merit badge.

It was Saturday. Kids were out playing. Lawns were being watered and I had till midnight to find a painting on Thirteenth Street.

Manny's was open for breakfast. Since it was a weekday and a little after eight in the morning, I had no trouble finding a parking space right on Hoover. Two days in a row. How lucky could I get?

Manny's Saturday breakfast crowd was there, including Juanita the fortune teller, who had an office in the Farraday. I liked Juanita, a shapeless sack of a woman who dressed as if she were trying out for a road company production of *Carmen*. Out of Juanita's overly painted lips sometimes came a zinger that made me think she might be the real thing.

She spotted me over her cup of coffee and said, "Give me one at Santa Anita, Peters."

"You're the fortune teller," I said, sitting next to her on a red leatherette stool.

"I can't use it for myself," she said. "I told you that. If I could use it for myself, you think I'd be half a month back on my rent?"

"No," I said.

She looked at me.

"You look like a wreck."

Manny had started a breakfast taco when he saw me walk through the door. Manny was a culinary master of impeccable taste. He always took the cigarette out of his mouth when he served a customer, and he changed his apron at least twice a month. He was about forty, dark, with a bad leg he claimed to have earned riding with Pancho Villa as a kid.

"She's right," said Manny, putting the breakfast taco, a black coffee, and a Pepsi in front of me.

"Spent a night in the Culver City lockup," I explained, picking up the taco and trying not to lose too much hot sauce, avocado, and egg. "Guy got murdered."

Manny handed me the morning paper and strolled back to the grill, a man of little curiosity. Nothing could match his adventures, real or invented, with Villa.

"A dead man will do it," Juanita said.

"What?"

"Someone's going to be killed by a guy name Guy," she said, looking into her coffee. I leaned over to see what was in the cup. Nothing but darkness and the same day-old java I was drinking.

"You talking to me?"

"Yeah," she said. "Someone's going to be killed by a guy named Guy or Greg in Mark's town. I just saw it in the coffee."

"Who killed the guy last night?" I asked, taking another bite of breakfast taco and nodding to Manny to get another. He was way ahead of me.

"How should I know?" Juanita said. "This stuff just comes."

I told her about the dead guy and the messages.

"Beats crap out of me," she said, getting off her stool while I took the last bite of taco and reached for the Pepsi. "I've got to get to work. Got three mothers coming. Kids, the soldiers, sailors, they don't come. They don't want to know what's going to happen to them. It's the mothers who want to know."

"What do you tell them?" I asked.

"Lies, usually," Juanita said. "Remember, Greg or Guy's going to do it in Mark's town. Oh yeah, this Greg or whatever has a beard."

She left and I read the paper and finished my coffee. The news was good. U.S. bombers were battering the

Japs on Wake Island, and the Russians were still pushing back the Nazis. Basil "The Owl" Banghart and Roger "The Terrible" Touhy were going to Alcatraz after escaping from Stateville in Illinois, where they were doing a long haul on kidnapping. There was a picture of Banghart in the paper. He did look a little like an owl.

I finished my breakfast, dropped a buck on the counter, and waved at Manny, who leaned back with his arms crossed and nodded, smoke curling up into his face as he dreamed of that last cavalry charge against Black Jack Pershing.

I could tell Jeremy had been up and at work as soon as I opened the outer door of the Farraday. The smell of Lysol was unmistakable. It's a smell I like. I like the smell of gasoline, too.

I went into the suite of Minck and Peters. Shelly wasn't there. His party hat sat on the dental chair as if he had melted and left only it and the odor of his last cigar. I went into my office, opened the window, sat down, and called my sister-in-law Ruth.

"How you doing, Ruth?" I asked cheerfully.

"Fine, Toby," she said.

"Happy New Year," I said.

"You know, don't you, Toby."

"Know? Know what?"

"You're brothers," she said lightly. "I could tell the way you said 'Happy New Year.' He told you? You saw him?"

"Yeah," I admitted. "I know people always say this but if there's anything I can do . . ."

"You can do a lot, Toby," she said. "You can come over here tomorrow for dinner. You can take the kids out to the park so I can spend some time with Phil. He's taking it hard."

"I know," I said. "Are you?"

"Taking it harder."

"It'll be all right," I assured her. "I told Phil I know a surgeon who'll know the right guy."

"Thanks, Toby," she said.

"They can take care of those things now," I said. "Army's developed all kinds of . . . hell, I don't know what I'm talking about, Ruth."

"Odds I've heard are about three-to-one in my favor," she said. "Before the war they were three-to-one against. I guess war is good for something. Gives doctors a lot of practice and a chance to experiment on dying men."

"Ruth—"

"I've been lucky, Toby. My husband was too old to be drafted and my sons are too young."

"I'll come by tomorrow at noon," I said. "That okay?"

"Fine," she said. "Toby, do you realize this is the longest conversation we've ever had?"

"Yeah, we finally had something to talk about."

She laughed on the other end and said, "Lucy wants to talk to you."

Lucy was Phil and Ruth's youngest, somewhere between two and three. When she was one she used to clobber me with her favorite toy, a Yale padlock.

"Uncle Toby?" came a small voice.

"Yes," I said.

"Moon is ca-ca," she said seriously.

"Sometimes I think you're right, kid," I said, and either Lucy or Ruth hung up.

Next call was to Doc Hodgdon, who was retired but still saw a few patients in his home. He wanted to know when we could get together for handball. I told him it would have to wait till I finished the case I was on. I told him about Ruth and he said he knew a few people. I gave him Phil and Ruth's number and promised to call him next week.

Then I made the call I dreaded. Barry T. Zeman answered the phone.

"It's me, Toby Peters," I said.

"Did you find them?" he said.

"I found one of the paintings and one of the clocks. Is Dali there?"

"They never leave the house," he said. "He doesn't like the outdoors. She goes running out when he needs something or she asks me to send my driver, J.T. The houseboy quit the second day they were here. The cook asked for a week off. Actually, he said he would be gone until the Dalis left. The housekeeper, who has worked for my family for thirty-eight years, has suddenly discovered an ailing relative in Lac Le Biche in Alberta, Canada."

"Life is hard," I admitted. "Can I talk to Dali? He's the client. He can fill you in."

He put the phone down and I waited. Gala came on.

"Yes?" she said eagerly.

"The Place in the note was a man named Adam Place. He's dead, murdered. The police have one of the paintings and one of the clocks. The killer, or maybe Place, ruined the painting and left a message."

I told her about Thirteenth Street and Dali came on the phone.

"Which painting?" he asked.

I described the painting.

"You must find the other ones."

I told him about Thirteenth Street.

"Ah," he said. "A mystical number. I once had a dream of a crystal with exactly thirteen sides floating in a hole in the head of a giant beast who sat on an enormous egg. I painted that image in a fit of rage in a single day and had to rest for a week."

"That's very helpful," I said.

"It is," he said with great seriousness, "alchemical. Find the other paintings. Find Gala's clocks. Find them.

My dreams are filled with fathers and the naked breasts of faceless women."

It could be worse, I thought, but I said, "A man's been murdered. Shot between the eyes. It might be a good idea to let the police know what's going on."

"No," said Dali.

That's not really accurate. He didn't say "no," he screamed. A nearly hysterical "*noooooooooooooooo.*"

"I'll get back to you as soon as I have anything," I said when the wail had played itself out.

"I am plagued," he wailed anew. "Who is this Wollowa Beckstine on the radio who they keep telling the time?"

"What?"

"It's five o'clock Wollowa Beckstine," he said solemnly.

"Bulova Watch Time," I explained.

"Bulova Watch Time," Dali repeated. And then, "Dali can't work."

"I'm sorry."

"Dali's work is an obligation, a burden." It was almost a sob. "Do you know how difficult it is to shock the world every twenty-four hours?"

"It's the curse of painters and politicians," I said.

"You are making a joke? You are joking at Dali?"

Gala took over the phone, her voice shaking. "Dali does not like to be the ass of jokes."

"The butt of jokes," I corrected.

"No, he says 'ass' of jokes. In the world of Salvador Dali, all jokes are made by Salvador Dali."

She hung up.

There is nothing like an appreciative client.

I went in search of Jeremy Butler. He'd solved the riddle of the first message for me. Maybe he could solve the second one in time for me to save a painting and maybe a life. Besides, I needed to hear a reasonably sane voice.

5

Most women would have been wary about answering a door to an apartment in a nearly empty downtown L.A. office building, but Alice Pallis did not hesitate. Alice feared neither man nor beast . . . nor robot. Alice was a formidable creature of no mean proportions who, less than a year ago, when she was still in the porno business, had hoisted a two-hundred-pound printing press and carried it four flights down the fire escape when the cops came calling.

When I stepped in, Natasha was lying on a blanket on the floor of the huge open room, which only a few months earlier had been brown, leather, musty, and filled with books. Since Alice and Jeremy had married, the room had brightened considerably. Alice had replaced all of the furniture with flowered sofas and a huge pink and purple rug covered the floor.

Natasha lay gurgling and playing with the pages of a thick blue-covered book.

"How's she doing?" I asked.

Alice smiled beautifully at her infant daughter. Natasha nibbled gently at the corner of the book.

"She absorbs," said Alice.

"What's she reading?" I asked.

"Fairy tales. Andersen. Jeremy believes that she should be surrounded by the proper books; that the words, the stories, come alive in the hands of one who is prepared to learn."

"You believe that?" I asked.

"I'm learning," she said.

"I need Jeremy."

"It's his meditation time," said Alice. "He's at Pershing Square. When he comes back he's going to read a fairy tale to Natasha."

Natasha stopped gnawing and looked up at me. She smiled. I left feeling a little better than when I had walked in.

Finding Jeremy was no great problem. I walked over to Pershing Square, which wasn't quite deserted, but it wasn't as crowded as it usually was, possibly because it looked like rain. A little guy who was shivering in spite of the eighty-degree temperature was standing on a box, a Chiquita Banana box, pounding his left fist into his right palm and shouting.

Jeremy and about five other men stood listening. Jeremy towered over the others and seemed to pay the most attention to the little guy. I started to say something to Jeremy; he put a finger to his lips to quiet me. I noticed a magazine under his arm. We turned to listen to the little man who was saying:

". . . and the first step will be a temporary prohibition of alcoholic beverages based on wartime need. That's the way the Eighteenth Amendment came last time, after the war, and they're talking about it again. Temporary will become permanent and the bootleggers, gangsters, and politicians will lobby to keep it that way, and the country will agree to keep it that way because it will add to the underground economy, and who will suffer?"

He looked around for an answer. The six of us didn't have an answer. Jeremy didn't drink and I was good for a Rainier beer about once a month. So the little guy answered for us.

"I'll suffer and people like you and me will suffer. The alcoholics, the winos. Drinking will go back to the middle classes. It'll be a game. For us it's a damn necessity and we're the ones who'll suffer. Now isn't some straight citizen out there going to tell me I'll be better off?"

He looked around for a straight citizen to do battle with him. Jeremy and I were the closest thing to it in the small group. No one wanted to mess with Jeremy.

"Not me," I said.

"Then amen to you, brother," said the little man, clutching himself as the first drops of rain came. One man in the small group shuffled off.

"It's not the government's job to save my life or tell me what's good for me," he said. "Why not ban smoking? Coffee? As long as I don't hurt you, you've got no right to hurt me."

Two more in the dwindling crowd went for shelter as the rain got a little more serious. The little man was shivering seriously now but he didn't plan to give up, though there were only three of us left.

"The brewers, the distilleries, they're going to fight it, but they lost before and they'll lose again. I'm going to run for Congress and in Congress I'm going to fight, scream, and filibuster for the right of every man to have a drink when he wants or to goddammit commit suicide with dignity if he wants."

The rain was serious now. The man next to Jeremy moved forward and helped the shivering little man from the box. He picked up the banana crate and led the little man toward the shelter of a store awning nearby. Jeremy and I moved the other way under the protection of a wind-blown tree.

"That man used to be a senator," he said, rubbing the sheen of water from his smooth head. "Not a state senator, a United States senator. Without conviction and cause he would be dead in a few months. Every man needs a joy of life or a sense of meaning."

"No quarrel with that," I said, and then as the rain imprisoned us in darkness against the trunk of the tree, I told him what had happened since I had last seen him.

"The streets in Santa Monica are numbered," I said. "But there is no Thirteenth there either. Thirteenth is Euclid."

"Spectator," Jeremy said pensively.

"You've got an idea," I said hopefully.

He took the magazine from under his arm and showed it to me. It was the latest issue of *Atlantic Monthly*. He flipped it open, found what he was looking for, and read to me:

"Houses have crumbled in my memory as soundlessly as they did in the silent films of yore."

He closed the magazine and looked at me.

"That's nice, Jeremy." I felt a chill creeping through my soaked windbreaker.

"It's in a short story by a young man named Vladimir Nabokov," he explained. "You have forgotten a house, Toby Peters."

"Can you help me remember, Jeremy?"

"It is never so meaningful as when one remembers oneself," he admonished.

"Then I'll regret my loss," I said. "While you're trying to improve my mind . . ."

"Your soul," he corrected.

"My soul," I accepted. "Another person could be murdered."

"Why does the note say 'Señor'?" asked Jeremy.

"The note's to Dali. He's Spanish," I said.

Jeremy shook his head sadly, patiently.

"The first note had 'Place' in capital letters," he said. "And this one has 'Street.'"

"So," I said, watching a woman dash across the street with a sheet of cardboard over her head. "Street is someone's name. Where? There aren't thirteen people named Street in the L.A. phone book."

"Señor," said Jeremy, "it is in the Town of the Spectator."

"Hollywood," I said.

"In Spanish, *spectator* is *mirador*," Jeremy explained.

"Holy shit. Jeremy, remember when we were in Mirador about a year ago on the Hughes case, the sheriff was . . ."

"Mark Nelson," said Jeremy.

A shot of thunder.

"I don't like things like this," I said. "I like it straight and simple. I don't like puzzles, and I sure as hell don't want to risk running into Nelson. What am I going to do?"

Jeremy looked down at me and said nothing.

"Right," I said. "I'm going to Mirador."

When the rain slowed enough to make it less than insane to do so, I headed back to the Farraday Building. When I got there, I put on a dry if not clean shirt I kept in my office and removed the .38 Smith & Wesson five-shot revolver I kept locked in the lower drawer. I almost never carried the gun. In the last five years, I had lost it three times, been shot by it once, and never used it to stop or even confront anyone threatening me. But now I was on the trail of a killer who was leaving clues like at a Crime Doctor movie, a killer who had made a third eye in the forehead of a taxidermist named Place and was ready to do something equally nasty to a citizen named Street.

I made it to the Crosley with a newspaper over my head, got in and headed for the Pacific Coast Highway. The skies grumbled, stayed gray but stopped raining as I did my best to keep from thinking. It didn't work. Try it some time.

Was someone killing people just because their names left interesting clues? Did Place have anything to do with the Dali theft? If there was a Street in Mirador, was he or she a part of this or just a poor sap who happened to have the right name?

An hour later I turned off the highway at the Mirador exit and two minutes later was on Main Street. I didn't know if Mark Nelson was still sheriff. I hoped I didn't have to find out. We hadn't gotten along like arms-around-the-neck buddies.

Downtown looked almost the same as it did the last time I had hit town. There were six store-front buildings on the main street. One of them was the sheriff's office, another was a restaurant named Hijo's. A place that used to sell "Live Bait" was now a hardware store, and three shops that used to be boarded up were now in business, though closed for the day. One of the shops, Old California, a few doors down from the sheriff's office, sold antiques. The second specialized in "New and Used Clothes" and the third was Banyon's Real Estate. The war boom had hit Mirador. There was no one on the street but a big guy in overalls looking into the window of the antique shop. Whatever was in there had his full attention. His face was flat against the window.

I kept driving till I came to a gas station I remembered. It was open. I got the kid on duty to fill the Crosley and went in to look at his phone book. The kid, tall and pimply with straight corn-colored hair and overalls, came in and said, "Eighty-three cents."

"How many people live in Mirador?" I asked.

He shrugged as I handed him a dollar.

"Keep the change," I said.

"Maybe a few thousand if you count the rich ones who only come in the winter," the kid said, pocketing the whole buck and putting nothing in the till.

"There are thirty listings in the phone book for people named Street," I said.

"Lot of Streets," he replied seriously.

The inside of the station was small, crowded with stacks of oil cans and old Dime Detectives. It smelled of gasoline and musty pulp magazines.

"Why?"

"Streets founded the place," he said. "My grandma on my ma's side is a Street."

"The thirteenth Street listed in the phone book is a Claude Street," I said. "On Fuller Drive. How do I get there?"

"Claude's probably in his shop," said the kid, picking up a comic book and sitting in a wooden armchair behind a battered desk covered with old issues of *Black Mask*. "Spends most of his time there now that the tourists are back."

"And where's his shop?" I tried.

"Passed it on the way in. Old California Antiques on Main Street."

I was going to say thanks and leave, but the kid put his comic book down and came up with a rifle from nowhere.

"Hands on your head," he said, standing.

I put my hands on my head.

"Why are you asking all these questions about Mirador?"

"I'm looking for Claude Str—"

"You a Jap spy? No, maybe you're a Nazi. Japs landed

you in a submarine. I've been watching the beach a year. So have Andy and Dad."

"I drove up in a car, remember?" I reminded him as he reached for the phone.

"Smart. I know you guys're smart. I know you got big subs," he said.

"Not big enough to hold a car," I tried.

"Big enough to hold that little Jap car," he said, nodding toward my Crosley.

"It's an American car. And how would they get it out of the submarine? Through the little trapdoor?"

This gave him pause.

"Smart," he said.

"I'm a private detective, undercover," I said. "Call the sheriff. Call Mark Nelson. He knows me."

Yeah, I thought, Nelson knows me. He told me never to come back to Mirador unless I wanted to go through life walking like a sloth on my knuckles.

"You know Sheriff Nelson?"

"Like a brother."

He lowered the rifle and took his hand away from the phone. I slowly took my hands away from my head, without asking permission.

"Sorry," the kid said. "Just that we've been expecting the Japs for two years. We're ready for them, too. I practice every Friday."

"Great," I said. "They usually land at night. Keep a flashlight handy and get them one by one as they come out of the little door."

The kid nodded, taking in this sage advice. I gave him another dime for a Whiz candy bar and a Pepsi from the refrigerator in the corner and got back in my Crosley.

Nothing was happening in the center of town and I felt less than comfortable parking near Sheriff Nelson's office, but no one appeared on the street when I got out and headed for the door of the Old California Antique

Shop. The guy in overalls who had been looking in the window was gone. I tried the door. Locked. I knocked. No answer. Through the window I could see shelves of curlicue lamps, clocks with gold-painted cupids, and fancy little boxes.

It looked like the kid was wrong and Claude Street wasn't at work. I couldn't blame him. Business on the street wasn't even good enough to be called bad. It wasn't raining but looked as if it might. The rich people were probably in their beach houses with their binoculars and hunting rifles, waiting for the invasion.

There was a narrow grassy space between the antique shop and the hardware store. It was worth a try. I walked between the buildings and found the back door of Old California. I didn't knock this time. I tried the handle. The door opened. I went in and closed it behind me.

I was in a back room, very dim. There were no windows, but there was a curtain across the door leading into the shop. The curtain was thin. I went in. A man, who for want of better information I took to be Claude, was lying on the floor, his legs sprawled across an overturned chair and a hole, a little bigger than the one in Adam Place's forehead, in his throat. On a table, ticking happily and watching over the scene, was Gala Dali's second clock. The glass face of the clock was broken and covered with blood. Over the clock, hanging from the wall was Dali's second painting, a grasshopper sitting on an egg. The egg was cracked and a small human head and arm were trying to get out. The grasshopper seemed to be looking down at the human and I had the feeling that when the little guy got out he'd be grasshopper food. There was something else in the painting—or had been until someone had splashed green over the lower right-hand third of the canvas. Written in yellow over the green was,

Time is running out. One clock. One painting.
Last chance. Look where he ate the sardine.

Claude was a slightly overweight man with a little yellow wig—I could tell it was a wig because it had fallen off when he fell—and round blue eyes locked on a not-very-interesting light fixture in the ceiling.

To be sure he was who I thought he was, I checked his pocket and found his wallet. He was Claude Street, all right. I took a closer look at the Dali painting and saw a bloody handprint like a signature in the lower left-hand corner. The blood was still wet. I looked at the floor, listened to the ticking of Gala Dali's clock, and let my eyes follow the trail of dripped paint to the curtain. I got my .38 in my hand, then moved to the curtain. I pushed the curtain aside and stepped into the front of the store. Nobody, at least nobody inside. Outside the window, standing in front of my Crosley, was the man I wished least to see, Sheriff Mark Nelson of Mirador.

Nelson was a wiry little man, about forty, in a lightweight white suit and a straw hat. He squinted at me through the window as if unsure of what he was seeing. I stood still. He moved right up to the window, took off his straw hat, shielded his eyes with his right hand, and looked at me and the .38 in my hand.

I considered my options, put the .38 back in my pocket and moved to open the front door of the Old California Antique Shop so the now-smiling sheriff could enter.

"Mr. Toby Peters, you are a trial and a tribulation," said Sheriff Nelson about five minutes later as he ushered me into his office two doors down from the Old California Antique Shop. "A trial and a tribulation. You were so on the occasion of our last meeting and you are once again."

The sheriff's office was a remodeled store about the

same size as the one run by the recently deceased Claude Street, but the layout was different. There was a low wooden railing with a gate. Visitors on one side. Cops and robbers on the other. Nelson held the gate open for me and I went in, past a desk and chair with a bulletin board behind them full of notes, clippings, and "Wanted" posters. To the left was a cubbyhole of an office with "Sheriff" marked on the door. To the right were two cells, both with open doors, neither occupied.

Nelson had my .38. He had taken it as soon as I had opened the door of the Old California Antique Shop. He had then walked through the curtain and seen Claude Street's body. It was when he came back through the curtain the gun in his hand aimed at my chest, that he first declared me "a trial and tribulation."

Nelson pointed to the first cell. I stepped in. He closed it behind me.

"There have been four murders in the history of this municipality," he said, shaking his head and looking constipated.

"The Indians probably killed each other from time to time before we came here," I suggested. "And the Spanish—"

"One of these murders, in 1930—" he went on.

"Woman on the beach brained her husband with a rock," I recalled.

Nelson smiled, a very pained smile.

"You have a memory worthy of remark," he said. "You are correct. The next murder we had was a little over one year ago and you were very much a thorn in my side during that episode. The third murder should not really count. A Mex farmer south of town shot a man who, he says, was engaged in an unappreciated folly with the Mex farmer's wife. And now this. Mr. Toby Peters, you have been involved in one-half of the murders which have taken place in Mirador since I became sheriff."

There was a cot in the cell. I remembered it had a lurking spring. I sat down on the cot and looked up at Nelson, who was wiping the inside band of his straw hat.

"I'm going to tell you something, sheriff," I said. "I know you won't do anything about it, but I'll feel better having said it. The person who killed Claude Street can't be far away. The paint on the picture and on the floor was still wet. He didn't have a car parked, at least not nearby. Mine was the only one out there till you pulled up."

Nelson moved to the chair at the desk and sat. He looked at the phone and then swiveled the chair with a screech like teeth against a blackboard and glared at me.

"I do not care for you, Mr. Peters," he said. "That you may have surmised from my demeanor. The Municipality of Mirador has grown in population and industry since you were last here. Murder most violent is not conducive to tourism."

"I noticed the boomtown excitement," I said.

"See, there you are. Sarcasm. Big city sarcasm." He plopped his straw hat on the desk and looked at the phone. "That's what people move down here to get away from."

"Nelson," I said. "Pick up the phone and call the Highway Patrol. This is out of your league."

"You are a truly vexing person," he said. "I will indeed call the Highway Patrol in a few moments—to inform them that I have apprehended the murderer of a member of one of Mirador's oldest families."

"Oldest," I repeated. "Not most prominent, most beloved?"

"Oldest will suffice," said Nelson, looking away from me through the front window of the office. Two kids, one boy, one girl, both about ten, were walking down the middle of the street unthreatened by Mirador's growth of population and industry. "And respected."

"Respected?"

"Any family which is capable of contributing one hundred and six votes in a town of a little more than two thousand permanent residents is a respected family," Nelson explained, letting his fingers touch the phone.

"One hundred and five," I corrected.

"One hundred and six is what I said and what I meant," Nelson said with irritation. "Mr. Claude Street was a newcomer to this community and had not yet registered to vote."

"Newcomer?"

"One who has recently come," Nelson said with a shake of his head, as if talking to a semi-retarded nephew, "from Carmel." He said "Carmel" as if it were a particularly sticky and unpleasant word.

"It was not easy to rent that store," he said.

"You own the store?"

"If it is of any concern to you, I own all of downtown," Nelson said, without enthusiasm. "And as you can see, it has made my fortune."

"Nelson, I didn't kill Claude Street," I said. "You know that."

His back was to me now and he was staring at the phone.

"I know no such thing," he said in total exasperation. "The evidence would suggest quite the contrary. I found you with a gun in your hand."

"It won't match the bullet in Street's neck."

Nelson's sigh was enormous.

"You could have shot him with another weapon that you disposed of or have hidden," he said.

"You've wasted a good five minutes."

"Do you know what I truly wanted to do with my existence?" he asked, picking up the phone and lifting the receiver off the hook. He turned to me quickly, and I shook my head to indicate that he had not previously shared this confidence with me—nor had I figured it from the many clues he had dropped.

Into the phone he said, "Miss Rita Davis Abernathy, will you please connect me with the office of the Highway Patrol . . . No, Miss Rita, you may not inquire . . . It is police business . . . I am confident that if you display even a modicum of patience and listen in on the line after you connect me—which I am as sure you will do as I am sure my mother's favorite child is sitting in this chair . . . Thank you, Miss Rita."

While he waited for Miss Rita to put him through, Nelson turned to me and remarked, "I wanted to be a man of the cloth, as my father was before me, and his father before him."

"Why didn't you?" I asked.

"I did not have the calling," he said.

"Amen," I said as into the phone he said, with great animation, "Lieutenant Freese? It is I, Sheriff Mark Nelson of the Municipality of Mirador. A homicide has taken place."

He looked at me again and continued, "It is likely that I have apprehended the person who committed the crime, but it is also possible that he had assistance or that . . . I will be happy to get to the point if you will; my father always said that a man should be allowed to finish what he . . . About ten minutes ago . . . I have no deputy on duty. As you may recall, I have only one deputy, Deputy Mendoza, who is using his day off to— Thank you."

He hung up the phone and turned to me again.

"What has happened to civility in this world?"

He pulled out his handkerchief and wiped his brow.

"A lost art," I sympathized.

"There is but one church in this town and the minister, alas, is without style or substance." Nelson stood up.

I knew—and Nelson knew—that he should go a few doors down and at least give the impression he knew what he was doing, but he didn't have the heart for it. In the long run, he was doing the right thing, staying out of the way till the Highway Patrol showed up.

"How few of us are fortunate enough to achieve our life ambitions," he said.

"It's better to have ambitions and not achieve them than to have none at all," I responded.

Nelson looked at me seriously for the first time since our eyes had met through the window of Claude Street's Old California Shop.

"First Corinthians?" he asked.

"*Charlie Chan in Rio,*" I answered.

Neither of us spoke again until the Highway Patrol car pulled up in front of the sheriff's office about twenty minutes later. I lay on the cot looking at the ceiling and Nelson sat looking out the window at the car from which two Highway Patrol officers in full uniform and as big as redwoods stepped out and looked around. There wasn't much to see.

Nelson was up, hat in hand, as phony a smile as I've seen anywhere but on the face of a receptionist at Columbia Pictures.

"It is not my day," Nelson said between his closed smiling teeth. "The Rangley brothers."

The two state troopers came in and moved past Nelson in my direction. One had a face like Alley Oop with a shave and the other one looked like his brother.

"Trooper Rangley," Nelson began. "This—"

"Where's the dead man?" interrupted the bigger Rangley.

"Two doors down," said Nelson. "In the Old California Antique Shop. His name is . . ."

But the Rangley's, after looking at me as if to say I was

one sorry specimen, turned and went back out on the street. They moved out of sight to the right of the window. Nelson turned to me. "I cannot but believe, though it runs counter to reason," he said, "that you have killed Mr. Claude Street for the sole purpose of bringing tribulation into my life."

"I didn't kill him, Nelson," I said.

Nelson's smile was gone.

"My lady is waiting for me," he said. "My fondest wish at this moment is to absent myself and allow the Rangley brothers—who, to the best of my knowledge, have no first names nor any need of them—to persuade you to confess to every crime committed within the state of California from moments after your birth to the instant I confined you to that cell."

"Here they come," I said.

Nelson put his smile back on and pivoted in his swivel chair to face the Rangleys as they came back into the sheriff's office.

"Man's dead in there," said the bigger Rangley.

"That was my conclusion upon witnessing the corpse," said Nelson.

There were two possible ways to interpret Sheriff Nelson's statement: He was either humoring these walking specimens of recently quarried stone, or he was making a joke he was confident would elude them. I would have voted for the former, but Rangley Number Two was taking no chances.

He was about a foot taller than Nelson. He stopped in front of him and smiled. Though I didn't think it possible, Nelson's smile got even broader.

Big Rangley was moving toward me in the cell. I kept sitting on the cot. His face was red and Alley Oop wasn't smiling at me.

"Sardines. 'Look where he ate the sardine'? I don't like crazy shit," he muttered softly.

Since I agreed with him, there wasn't much for me to say. I nodded. "The other officer over there behind me," he went on, "he's my brother. He likes crazy shit even less than I do."

The other brother was losing the grinning battle with Nelson, though I knew the sheriff was doomed to lose the war.

The big Rangley said, "Keys."

Sheriff Nelson pulled his keys out and handed them to the patrolman, who threw them to his brother, who, without removing his brown eyes from me, held up his hand to catch them. The keys flew past him and landed inside the cell at my feet.

"All the good receivers were drafted," I said, reaching down for the key ring.

It was the wrong thing to say.

"Just pick up the keys and open the cell," he said. "Officer Rangley and the sheriff are going a few doors down to wait for the evidence truck and the county coroner while you and I palaver."

I swear he said "palaver," but the way he said it convinced even me that I'd be better off playing second banana in this Kermit Maynard western.

"The prisoner is—" Nelson began.

"—about to be interrogated," said the big Rangley as his brother ushered Nelson to and through the front door.

I got up and opened the door. Rangley came around the corner and entered. He put out his hand and I gave him the key.

"Been locked up before?" he asked.

"A few times. Once before in this cell."

"Tell me about sardines," he said.

"Not much to tell," I answered. "When I was a kid I liked to make sardine salad—mash up a can with onions and mayo. Still like it once in a while. Or a sandwich on white with butter and a thick slice of onion."

Rangley nodded, muttered something like "hmmpff" and closed the cell door. The keys went into his pocket.

"This came at a bad time . . ."

"Peters," I said. "Toby Peters. I'm a private investigator. I was—"

". . . about to sit," said Rangley.

I sat on the cot.

"You know there're springs in that cot?" he said, standing over me.

"Yes," I said.

He looked around the cell and shook his head.

"Even a half-assed short-timer could pull a spring at night and cut the eyes off Nelson or his homo Mex deputy," he went on.

"That's an idea," I said.

He laughed and the heel of his right hand came forward and slammed against what was left of my nose. That wasn't too bad, but I flew back on the cot and hit my head on the wall. That was bad. I rebounded and thought I heard a musical saw.

"How's the head?" he asked gently, handing me his pocket handkerchief.

"Fine," I said, accepting the handkerchief and putting it to my nose.

"Don't worry about the blood," he said with a smile, sitting next to me. "Can I give you a little advice?"

"You have my undivided attention."

He put his hand on my knee and whispered, "Don't answer me smart again."

"That's good advice," I said, checking the handkerchief. It was wet and dark red.

"Keep it," he said gently.

"Thanks," I said.

"You kill the guy?"

"The one with the yellow wig?"

"Is there more than one?"

"I just saw the one," I said.

"How's your head?" he asked again, touching my arm. I got the point.

"I didn't kill him. I was trying to find him. Someone stole three Salvador Dali paintings and three clocks from my client."

"Three clocks, three paintings," he repeated with a knowing nod of the head. "Big clock in there one of the clocks?"

"Yeah."

"And that painting? That grasshopper on the egg crap in there. That one of the paintings?"

"Right," I said.

"This Dali's a crazy asshole," he said.

"That could be," I said, putting the handkerchief back to my nose.

Big Rangley chuckled. I didn't know what was funny but, as Wild Bill Elliot says, I'm a sociable man. I made a sound that might well be taken for a chuckle.

"Remember what I said when I came in this place, Peters?"

"You don't like crazy shit."

"Don't like it at all," he agreed, clapping me on the back. He reached into his vest pocket and came out with a little notebook, which he flipped open to the first page and read:

"Time is running out. One clock. One painting. Last chance. 'Look where he ate the sardine.'"

He closed the notebook, returned it to his vest pocket and buttoned it.

"Now," he said. "What the hell does that mean?"

"I don't know," I said.

Beyond the window a Mirador crowd was gathering. A

crowd in Mirador was somewhere between two and six people. This crowd included two girls around ten, the kid from the gas station where I had used the phone book, and a vacant-looking fat man in overalls whose palms and nose were pressed to the window the way they had been pressed against the antique shop window when I had driven down Main Street about an hour ago. Another car pulled up at the curb. The crowd turned and a man about seventy got out of a black Ford coupe. He came to the door of the sheriff's office, opened it and saw Rangley.

"Two doors over, Doc," said Rangley, pointing past me. "Melvin's in there."

Doc was wearing a wrinkled long-sleeved blue shirt and suspenders, no tie. He was carrying one of those black doctor bags. Doc looked at me.

"Don't hit him again, Beau," the doctor said and left the office, closing the door behind him.

"Doc's a humanitarian," Rangley confided. "But Doc doesn't have to talk to many living people during business hours. Easy to be a humanitarian when you don't have to meet humanity."

"Trooper," I said. "You're a philosopher."

"And you're one hell of a fool if you think what the doc said and those village half-wits out there watching are going to stop me from ripping what's left of your nose off if you smart off."

The punch was low, short, and hard. It caught me about where my kidney must be.

"I didn't kill him," I said, trying to keep the pain from my voice.

I knew the next question and my next answer. I considered throwing an elbow into Trooper Beau Rangley's throat. It might work, but what then? A run for L.A. in my Crosley? I tightened my muscles, those that would still pay attention, and waited.

"Who you working for, Peters?"

I looked at the retarded man with his face against the window. He grinned at me. It was a nice friendly grin. He pulled his left hand from the window. It left a bloody handprint.

"I can't tell you that without the client's permission," I said, forcing myself to look at Rangley and not at the window.

The outer door to the sheriff's office came open before Rangley could throw the punch, and his brother came in with Sheriff Nelson.

"Doc wants to see you, Beau," Mel Rangley said.

Beau smiled and stood up. He straightened the creases in his brown uniform and gently slapped my cheek. He got blood on his palm.

"We'll talk again in a few minutes," he said, moving to the cell door and opening it.

I kept my mouth shut until Beau and Mel were out the door. The crowd, except for the retarded man, followed them in the direction of the Old California Antique Shop.

"You see," said Nelson, pointing his hat at me.

I wasn't sure what it was I was supposed to see, but I doubted Nelson planned to explain and I knew I didn't care. He sat in his chair and swiveled so that his back was to me again. He looked up at the retarded man and shouted, "Martin Sawyer, you are, as you have been for the past thirty-five years, looking through the wrong window."

Nelson pointed to his right; the retarded man watched with curiosity and no understanding.

"Nelson," I said. "I didn't do it."

Nelson swung around and looked at me.

"Well," he said with a deep sigh. "I am relieved. Why did you not make that clear to me when I first found you, gun in hand? I think I'll just let you out and apologize."

"I want a lawyer," I said.

"You will have to take that up with the troopers Rangley," he said.

"I'm *your* prisoner," I reminded him.

"I have washed my hands of the whole—Martin Sawyer, get the hell away from that window."

We were at this crucial point in the conversation when the Rangleys and the doctor came back in, leaving their audience outside.

"Peters," said the senior Rangley, "when did you get to Mirador?"

"About an hour ago, maybe an hour and a half," I said.

"And," he went on, "you went right to the antique shop?"

"No, I got gas from that kid, the one standing out there on the sidewalk. The pimply one with the overalls."

"He told us," said Rangley.

"I'm going back to the body," said the old doctor wearily.

"Hold your horses," said Rangley, holding up his hand. Then to me, "Where were you last night, between—"

"Midnight to five or so," said the doctor. "That's safe enough."

"Culver City lockup," I said, standing up. "From about eleven to nine in the morning."

"Go check it, Mel," Rangley said. His brother nodded and went out the door. I watched him muscle through the watching kids and head for the car.

"I'm going back," said the doc. He turned and went back to the street, leaving me, Nelson, and the trooper who hated puzzles.

No one spoke for a while. Nelson sat. Rangley stood and I held onto the bars with one hand and used my other one to dab my bloody nose with Rangley's handkerchief. My head hurt but I decided to put on a happy face.

Mel Rangley came running back in about two minutes. "He was in the Culver City lockup," Mel said.

I grinned broadly and threw the bloody handkerchief to Beau Rangley, who wasn't ready for it. The balled piece of cloth hit his neatly pressed shirt, leaving a dark, deep spot, and fell to the floor.

"Sorry," I said pleasantly.

"I think you'd better come with us," he said. "We've got a few more questions to ask you. Somewhere quiet. Let him out, Nelson."

Nelson put his straw hat on his head and swiveled toward Rangley.

"I think not," he said.

Rangley shook his head as if the world were a series of unexpected little heartbreaks that had to be endured.

"Open it," he repeated.

"No," said Nelson, standing.

Rangley was not looking at the sheriff, but I was. I could see the tremor in his knees, the twitch of his jaw, and the determination in his eyes.

"Nelson, one half-hearted piss and you'd flush down the toilet."

"Given the information provided by the good doctor, the confirmation of presence by the Culver City police and your obvious hostility toward the prisoner," said Nelson, "I do not believe it is in the best interest of the laws of the State of California and the Municipality of Mirador to release the prisoner to you. And that I do not intend to do."

Rangley turned to the sheriff and took three steps till they were nose to forehead. Nelson quaked and almost lost his straw hat, but he didn't back down.

"You're one simple shit, Nelson," Rangley hissed.

"That is as it may be," Nelson agreed, "but Peters remains in my charge."

With that Trooper Rangley stormed out the door and went to join his brother in their car. The small crowd turned to watch them drive off.

"Thanks," I said as Nelson's knees began a serious wobble. He made it back to his chair and grasped the arms as he sat heavily.

"There comes a moment when one least expects it that dignity takes precedence over survival," he said. "That is a moment to be watched for and avoided or one runs the risk of losing a secure job with a pension."

"What now?" I asked.

The crowd on the street was still there but it had dwindled to three, including the retarded man who had now fixed his gaze on me. I waved to him. He waved back and Doc appeared behind him, started toward his car, changed his mind, and entered Nelson's office, closing the door behind him.

"Street was killed by a gunshot," he said. "I've recovered the bullet. Death took place last night or early this morning. I called Hal Overmeyer. He'll bring the corpus to San Plentia Hospital and I'll play with it till I know more."

Doc looked at me and shifted his black bag to his other hand.

"Want me to look at your nose?" he asked.

"I'll be peachy," I said.

"Any other wounds need tending?" he asked. "I usually have to do a little patching in the wake of the Rangleys."

My head was throbbing and the ache in my side sucked deep and sharp.

"I feel great," I said. "Trooper Rangley knows how to treat a fella."

Doc looked at me and shook his head.

"Never that simple, mister," he said. "Beau and Mel are the last of the Rangley brothers. Rick died on Guam. Sam got killed in Morocco on a tank. And Harry, well, they never found enough of him to make it official. The oldest brother, Carl, he took a broken beer bottle in the gut half a year before the war broke out. Beau and Mel are draft-free and they promised their mother they wouldn't join. So, every time they're introduced to a new friend like you, they make 'em welcome. Rangleys are none too brilliant. You know what *sublimate* means?"

"No," I said. "Let me guess. They feel better when they kick someone's teeth out."

"Something like that," Doc agreed. "But to give you your due, the Rangleys weren't a friendly bunch even when there was an even half dozen of them. Sheriff Nelson, what say you let the innocent man out and all of us go over to Hijo's and have a few beers before my date with the deceased?"

Nelson's legs were back, at least back enough for him to nod and get up.

"Why not?" he said wearily. "I've got to give my wife a call first."

Doc took the keys from Nelson and moved toward me as Nelson picked up the phone.

"One more painting?" Doc asked as he opened the cell door.

"One more clock," I added, stepping into the office where Nelson was whispering into the receiver.

"Running out of time," said Doc, looking at the keys.

I looked out the window at the retarded man, who was still watching me with a happy grin. This was probably the most exciting day of his life.

"There was fresh blood on the floor of the antique shop," I said low enough so Nelson couldn't hear me from across the room.

"Not the victim's," said Doc. "Probably not the killer's either. I'd imagine whoever did it was long gone and far away before dawn."

I pointed to the window. Doc looked where I was pointing and saw the handprint.

We moved past Nelson's desk. The sheriff gave us a shrug, turned his back to us and continued whispering into the phone.

"Martin Sawyer," I said, looking at the retarded man.

Doc looked up as we reached the door.

"Like many of the inhabitants of Mirador, I delivered him."

"Harmless?"

"Harmless," said Doc, stepping out onto the sidewalk and holding the door open for me.

Nelson, still on the phone, waved us ahead.

We were standing in front of Martin Sawyer now, and Sawyer turned from the sheriff's office window and smiled gently at us as Doc sighed.

"Let me look at your hand, Martin."

Martin took his right hand out of his pocket and held it out. It was pink with flecks of fast-drying blood.

"Peters," said Doc, looking at the hand. "Martin Sawyer is incapable of committing violence."

"But not of witnessing it."

Through the window we could see Sheriff Nelson hang up the phone.

"I'd prefer that Martin not go through the pain of arrest and questioning," said Doc, guiding Martin's hand back to the overall pocket.

"I know who killed him," said Martin Sawyer happily. His voice was soft and high.

Nelson was moving toward the door through which Doc and I had just come.

"Who?" asked Doc.

"Last night, Mr. Claude told me a name. Then I came back before and Mr. Claude was, was, was . . ."

"Dead," I said.

Martin Sawyer looked frightened. His eyes moved to Sheriff Nelson, who was coming out of the door.

"What was the name Mr. Claude told you, Martin?"

"Gregory Novak," said Martin. "Mr. Claude said, 'Gregory Novak wants to kill me, but I'll fool him.'"

"What?" asked Nelson. "Martin Sawyer, go home to your sister. There is nothing here for you."

Sawyer rubbed his head and looked at Nelson.

"Gregory Novak," he said.

Nelson shook his head and pushed past Sawyer, heading toward Hijo's bar.

"Martin just told us that Claude believed someone named Gregory Novak was planning to kill him," said Doc.

"Hold it," I put in. "Juanita said someone would be killed by a guy called Guy or Greg, a guy with a beard."

"Juanita?" asked Doc.

"Fortune teller in L.A.," I explained.

Sheriff Nelson stopped, his back to us, paused for a beat and turned to look at the three of us.

"Gentlemen," said Nelson, "I anticipate both an eventful confrontation with my spouse and a future of less than cordial social interaction with the brothers Rangley. The respite of a bottle or two of Drewery's will be most welcome. It is my opinion that Gregory Norvell—"

"Novak," Martin Sawyer corrected helpfully.

"Novak," Nelson said with a weary sigh. "I stand corrected. It is my opinion that Gregory Novak is the name of a character on *Mr. Keen* or some other radio show which Martin Sawyer is unable to separate from reality. Now, I am going into the Mex bar and have a beer. Your companionship would be welcome, but it would not be the first time I have had a beer by myself."

Doc touched Martin Sawyer's arm and told him softly to get in Doc's car and wait for him. Then we joined Nelson in the bar.

6

At a table, one of four in Hijo's, Doc gave me a handful of aspirin for my head. I downed them with a bottle of some unknown and unnamed yellow liquid with a faint taste of beer. We sat drinking while Sheriff Nelson brooded over life, his wife, and the brothers Rangley. The radio behind the bar played a Treasury War Bond show. Jane Froman and Lanny Ross sang a duet—"This Love of Mine"— followed by a sketch with Betty Grable and Preston Foster as a married couple trying to get ready for a dinner while their maid, played by Joan Davis, gave them a hard time.

I got on the road as soon as I could and headed north. The Crosley wasn't in a hurry and my head had a lump the size and shape of a yucca leaf. I pulled in at South Carlsbad Beach just before Oceanside, had a hot dog at a shack called Hernie's, looked at the ocean and a white wooden naval lookout tower on stilts. I sat on a piece of driftwood and helped the tower look for the Japanese armada for about an hour. When I got up, my head throbbed and my back twinged, but it could have been worse.

I passed San Juan Capistrano as the sun was going down. The written history of California began at the Mission San Juan Capistrano. History was the one subject I had enjoyed in high school. In my one year and a little more at the University of Southern California, the only class I could pay attention to was history. I remembered one afternoon when Father Zephpyrin Engelhardt, the historian of the California Missions, had come to class complete with dark robes tied with a white rope and a little black skullcap on his head. He had a long white beard and carried an ancient book. I'd looked up Father Z in 1936 on my way through San Juan Capistrano, but he had died two years earlier.

It was Father Z who told us how California got its name. Father Z said, I've still got the notes somewhere, that a novel called *Las Sergas de Esplanadian—The Adventures of the Esplanadian*—by Garcia de Montalvo had been published in Spain in 1510. In the novel, which Father Z had read, there's a fantastic island of wealthy Amazons. For reasons which no one knows, Montalvo called the island *California*, a word he never defined. A word, in short, which has no meaning.

No one knows for sure how the western coast of North America picked up the name. It might have come with Spanish explorers in the sixteenth century. I like to think it came with Hernando Cortez, who conquered Mexico and spent some time slaughtering Aztecs in the Baja. It might have come with Juan Cabrillo, who in 1542 landed near what became San Diego.

It wasn't till more than two hundred years later, in August 1769, that some Spanish missionaries and soldiers made an expedition north and found a valley. They made camp by a river. Friendly Gabrielino Indians brought them gifts of shell beads and the next day the Spaniards moved on. They were the first non-Indians to spend a night in what is now downtown Los Angeles.

I stopped following the path of the missionaries into Los Angeles and headed for my brother's house in North Hollywood. Nothing was open but I stopped at a park I knew and picked some flowers.

When I got to the house, I knocked and Ruth answered.

"It's still Sunday," I said.

She smiled and I handed her the flowers.

"Thanks, Toby," she said, kissing my cheek as we stepped in.

The radio was on. A voice I recognized said something about U.S. bombers battering the Japanese on Wake Island.

Ruth was wearing a short-sleeved white-and-purple dress with fluffy shoulders. Her yellow hair was pulled back and tied with a purple ribbon. Strands were creeping out all over the place. She didn't look sick, but it wasn't easy to tell with Ruth, who was swizzle-stick thin and pale at the best of times.

"Kids up?"

"I told them this morning you'd be coming," she said, leading me through the small living room. An ancient photograph of my mother and father sat on top of the radio, which was now telling us to smoke Old Gold because it was lowest in irritating tars and resins and lowest in nicotine.

"From coast to coast," the voice said happily, "the swing's to new Old Gold."

We moved into the small kitchen, where Phil was sitting at the table over a bowl of cereal. A box of Wheaties sat next to his bowl. Cereal was the one passion we shared. Phil was still wearing his rumpled suit. His tie was loosened. He didn't say anything.

"Look what Toby brought me." Ruth said.

Phil paused in his crunching, looked at the flowers, and said, "Pretty."

"You'd better see the kids before they're asleep," Ruth said. "Phil will get you a bowl."

As we left the kitchen, Phil made a grunting noise and pushed his chair back. We went to Lucy's room first. Lucy was somewhere between waking and sleep. She blinked at me and clutched her stuffed rabbit. We moved to the boys' room. Both Nat and Dave were in bed but awake.

"Uncle Toby," said Dave, sitting up. "You were supposed to be here to take us to see Abbott and Costello."

"Couldn't help it," I said with shrug. "I was in jail."

"He's kidding," said Nat.

"No," I said. "I found a dead guy and the sheriff arrested me. Then a state trooper named Rangley hit me in the back of the head. Here, have a look."

Nat looked. Dave reached over to touch my lump.

"I wish I could have seen," Dave said. "Uncle Toby, all the good stuff happens to you."

"I've got to go talk to your dad," I said. "Let's shoot for Abbott and Costello next Saturday."

"If you're not in jail," Nat said cynically.

"Or dead," added Dave cheerfully.

"Good-night, men." I followed Ruth back into the hall and she closed their door.

"Phil just got home," Ruth said. "Can you keep it friendly tonight, for me?"

"Friendly," I said. "For you."

"Go sit down. I'll get something for your head."

Phil was probably on his fourth or fifth bowl of Wheaties when I joined him. He was looking down at the *L.A. Times*. He had prepared a bowl for me. I poured milk and took a spoonful.

"A guy got killed in Mirador," I said, looking at Phil.

He didn't look up, but said, "Claude Street, antique dealer. Another painting. Odd bullet like the one in Adam Place. State troopers want us to keep an eye on you. They don't think it's a coincidence that you found two bodies in two days under very similar circumstances."

Ruth came back in with a washcloth. She looked at both of us to be sure that the only violence in the room was being done to flakes of wheat.

I kept eating while Ruth worked on my head. Around a mouthful of cereal I said, "Killer may be a guy named Gregory Novak."

Phil pushed his bowl away, put down his paper, shook his head and looked at me.

"You got that from some poor half-wit named Sawyer. There isn't any Gregory Novak in Mirador. Seidman checked phone books for most of California. We've even checked the Armed Forces lists. We found two Gregory Novaks. One is blind, eighty-two, and crazy. But he has one arrest. A year ago for smoking cow shit."

"That's stupid, but is it a crime?" I asked.

Phil didn't bother to answer.

"He lives in Bakersfield. The other one is a petty officer on a destroyer somewhere in the Pacific."

"How's that feel?" Ruth queried.

My head felt wet and the bowl of water was pale red from my dried blood. It was my turn to push a bowl away. I got up and gave Ruth a quick kiss on the cheek.

"When—?" I began.

"Tomorrow," she said. "The next day. As soon as they can get me in. I'll let you know. I'll be all right."

"I'm sorry I couldn't get here. Hey, how about I pick

up the kids, all three of them, after school on Wednesday?"

"You're not taking Lucy anywhere," Phil growled.

"I'll watch her."

My eyes met Phil's and I could see the accusation. He sat there, creeping fast toward sixty, with three kids, a sick wife, and a mortgage. He looked at me with a history of half a century of my screwing up.

"Trust me," I said.

"I do," said Ruth, touching my arm. "You come and get them after school Wednesday."

Phil opened his mouth to say something but changed his mind. I finished my Wheaties and got up.

"I'll let myself out," I said. "Thanks."

Ruth sat where I had been. I touched her shoulder and headed for the living room. Two actors on the radio were talking tough about a woman named Hershvogel. Since the actors were whispering and my brother wasn't, I heard Phil, in the kitchen, say, ". . . because he's about as responsible as a brain-damaged oyster."

I looked at my parents' photograph on the radio. I had the feeling they agreed with Phil.

The price of gas, tire rationing, and the black-out kept the streets reasonably clear at night, but it still took me almost an hour to get to Beverly Hills and Barry Zeman's house on Lomitas. It was almost ten and I needed a shave and some clean underwear. I tidied my windbreaker, jauntily zipped it half way up and rang the bell.

The double Amazon woman I'd seen the last time I'd been there answered the door. She was about forty, a six-foot-tall left tackle with short yellow-white hair and very serious brown eyes. She wore a white uniform and a little white hat.

"Someone sick?" I asked.

"I'm not a nurse," she answered. "You have business here?"

"I'd like to see Dali or his wife," I said, knowing that I had no chance of bulling past her.

"They are not available," she said, her arms folded over her more than ample breasts.

"Tell them Toby Peters is here with another murder to report," I said with as pleasant a smile as I could put on my grizzly face.

"I don't care if you're President Franklin D. Gimp," she said. "The Dalis are not available."

"How about Zeman?"

"Not home, leave."

"You have a way with words, Miss . . . ?"

"Get the hell out of here," she said, starting to close the door.

"Miss Get-the-hell-out-of-here," I answered, putting my foot in the door. "I've had one shit of a day."

She kicked at my shoe, which was what I wanted. Instead of resisting I pulled my foot back, braced myself, and pushed against the door, which shot back and hit Miss Get-the-hell-out-of-here flat in the chest. She staggered and I stepped in, kicking the door shut behind me.

I didn't like the look on her face as she pulled herself together. My .38 was in my hand now.

"Let's be friends," I suggested.

She took a step toward me.

"I'm holding a gun," I said, pointing to the gun.

This made no impression on her. She was about a foot from my face and towering over me. I could either kill her or have the crap kicked out of me by a woman of no mean proportions.

"Odelle," came a voice from my right as the woman grabbed my wrist. It hurt like hell.

"I'm just going to kill him a little," Odelle said, breathing a combination of garlic and Sen-Sen in my face.

"Odelle," Dali repeated. "Death offends and frightens

me. It is not inspiring. No one, with the possible exception of one's father, should ever die. Do you agree, Mr. Toby?"

"Completely," I said, trying to pry Odelle's hand from my wrist. My hand was numb and the gun was about to fall out of fingers quickly losing their feeling.

Odelle released my hand. I fumbled the .38 back into my holster and turned to Dali, who was posed on the staircase in a crimson velvet cape with a leopard-skin collar.

"Odelle," he said, pointing at the woman, "is a model."

"Great," I said.

"There," said Dali, pointing toward the living room. I looked where he was pointing and saw a canvas on an easel in the middle of the room. Painted on the canvas was a melting clock. Behind the clock was a naked woman whose back was turned. The woman's shoulder was made of stone and little pieces were cracking off and tumbling toward the ground like tears of flesh. The woman, even from behind, looked nothing like Odelle.

"She pose for the clock?" I asked.

"Odelle is all women," he said, stepping into the living room to admire his work. I followed him, Odelle uncomfortably close behind. I'd seen a clock like the one in the painting, in Place's place and Street's antique shop, but this clock was as runny as a Wilbur Bud candy on an August afternoon.

"Beautiful," I said with my best touch of sarcasm.

"I could not paint the clock until there were no clocks," he said, turning toward me and opening his eyes wide. "If you bring the clocks back, I will be unable to paint them. I do not paint from life. Life has no meaning."

"Then why do you have little Odelle pose for you?"

"Odelle, I told you, is not a single woman. She is an abstraction. All women. The clocks are singular."

"Makes sense to me," I said.

The wavy hands of the clock in the painting said it was three-thirty. Since the clock was melting, the bottom of the clock was visible and I could see something written in gold letters in a language that looked like . . .

"Russian," said Odelle in my ear.

Her voice was filled with awe.

"You were looking at the words on the clock," she went on. "They're Russian."

"My paintings?" Dali asked.

"Another man's been murdered," I said. "Man named Claude Street. You know the name? Until he decided to move to Mirador to die, he lived in Carmel. Antique dealer."

Dali touched his nose. "No. I do not know . . ."

"How about Gregory Novak?" I tried.

"Gregory Novak? No," he said, moving to a fashionable Louis the Somethingth chair in front of the painting.

"How about Mrs. Dali?"

"I know her," Dali said, looking at me with a smile and a raise of his eyebrows.

"Sal," I said, looking down at Dali, "I am not in the mood for jokes. People are dead and I'm tired. I need the money but I don't think I like you. I'm quitting. I'll send you a bill and a report tomorrow."

Odelle was suddenly between me and the painter.

"You do not talk to Mr. Dali like that," she said very, very softly.

"Yes I do, Odelle. And if you touch me again, this time I will shoot you."

I grinned at her and Dali said, "Odelle, Odelle, Odelle. You are a porcelain vase. You are not a . . . a . . . *maleante*, a . . ."

". . . thug," Gala supplied from the steps.

She stepped into the room, a tiny wraith in a leopard-skin cape with a crimson velvet collar, and moved to her husband. She took his hand and patted it reassuringly.

"He talks of murder," Dali said, dragging the word *murder* out into three syllables.

"Dali doesn't like to hear of death," Gala said, turning to me. Odelle moved out of the way. "Death is not surreal."

"I'm going home," I said.

"You must find Dali's painting, my clocks," Gala said, stepping in front of me as I moved toward the door.

"The Highway Patrol has one of your clocks. Culver City police have another, and I don't know where the hell the third one is."

Gala looked puzzled.

"Ah," said Dali behind me. "Sardines. Yes."

"Where did you eat sardines?" I asked, turning back to him.

"I hate sardines," he said with a shudder, hugging himself. "I painted a can of sardines once because they came to me unbidden in a dream. I do not eat sardines."

"In Carmel," Gala said. "At the party when we moved in. You ate one on a cracker. Odelle, you remember, you were—"

"No!" shouted Dali, shaking his head. His hair went wild and his long pointed mustaches quivered. "That never happened."

"It never happened," Gala agreed. "Mr. Toby Peters, find Dali's painting."

I looked at Odelle, whose eyes were moist with concern. Those eyes, which a minute earlier were dripping blood, were moist and begging me for mercy.

"You got a Pepsi here?" I asked. "Or a beer?"

"Odelle," said Gala, and Odelle went clumping off down the hall.

"Why would anyone kill two guys, leave goofy clues, and ruin two of your paintings?"

"He is an artist," Dali tried, pointing a finger toward the ceiling. "You must find the last painting. If it is not returned . . ."

"And the clocks," Gala added.

"Cops in Culver City have one of the clocks. Cops in Mirador have another. The only way you're going to get them back is to admit they're yours, and then the cops start asking you questions. You want to go down to the Wilshire Station and answer questions?"

"But it was only a . . . a . . . *chiste*," said Dali.

"A joke?" I said. "What are you . . . ?"

"Tell him," said Dali, smoothing down his hair.

Gala looked at her husband, then at the painting, and then at me as Odelle trotted back in the room, spilling beer from a cup shaped like an inverted skull. She held it out to me. I took it and drank deep while Gala Dali made up her mind.

"Dali," she said to her husband, "this time you have gone too far."

"It's the only place I ever wanted to go," Dali replied.

"A man," Gala said, turning to me. "We paid him to take the two paintings. We were going to call the newspapers and tell them about it and give interviews, but he took three paintings and the clocks and now people are being murdered. That does not please Dali."

I finished the beer and handed the empty glass to Odelle, who took it gratefully.

"I can understand that," I said. "You think you can tell me something about this guy? Novak, right?"

"Novak?" Gala looked at me curiously. "No, his name was Taylor."

"How did you find this Taylor?"

"He . . ." Gala began, but before she could finish a bullet shattered the window and blew a hole in the middle of the back of the naked woman in Dali's painting. I jumped for Dali and pushed him out of the chair and to the floor.

"Get on the floor," I called back to Gala and Odelle, who stood there in a trance. Odelle held the empty skull cup in front of her.

The second shot went into and through the chair in which Dali had been sitting a few seconds earlier.

"Turn off the goddamn lights, then," I shouted.

Odelle moved to the light switch; Gala let out a scream and dropped down toward Dali and me on the floor. The third shot missed her, but not by much. The lights in the living room went out as Odelle galloped into the hall and hit the switch.

Darkness. No more bullets. Dali was mumbling something in Spanish. Gala answered him in French. They were both holding onto me.

I got free and crawled to the shattered window. In the darkness I could hear someone running away from the house.

"Stay down," I warned, getting to my feet and going for the door. My leg was sending desperate signals that running was not one of my options. Whoever fired at Dali was on foot. Maybe I could get in my car and find him before he got to his car, assuming he was going for a car and wasn't one of the neighbors who'd had enough of the Dalis.

A car pulled into the driveway. I opened the front door. Behind me, somewhere in the dark, I could hear Odelle hyperventilating like the Twentieth Century Limited. Barry Zeman, complete with tux and black tie, was getting out of a Stutz Bearcat.

"Peters?" he asked.

"Peters it is," I said, moving for my car.

"What happened?" he asked, looking at the broken window and the darkened house.

"No time," I said. "Dali will tell you."

I crawled into the passenger side of my car and shuffled over to the driver's seat.

"Where was Jim running?" he asked through my open window.

"Jim?" I echoed, turning on the ignition.

"Jim Taylor, J.T., my chauffeur," he said, looking toward the street. "I just saw him running from the house."

"Was he carrying anything?"

"Yes, I think so."

"Which way?" I asked, inching the car past him.

Zeman pointed to the left.

"What—?"

"Later," I said, clanking into the night.

Downhill, wide open on a flat road with nothing coming, the Crosley could hit forty miles an hour. But I wasn't in that kind of a hurry. I turned left on the street. I didn't know what Taylor looked like; I'd only seen him from the back in the garage the day before, when I first met the Dalis. But there weren't many people walking the streets of Beverly Hills at this hour, and the guy I wanted was carrying a rifle or something big enough to hold a rifle.

I coaxed the Crosley into doing its best. I didn't want to panic Taylor. I wanted to spot him, slow down, follow him till I could nail him just before he got in his car.

I almost missed him. There aren't any cars parked on Beverly Hills streets—you park in the driveway or the garage. Only intruders park on the street, and the cruising cops are on them before they can get an autograph or break into Fred Astaire's pantry.

A few parties were going on, with cars parked in their respective driveways. I crept past the second party I came to in time to observe a Ford parked behind a white Rolls back into the street. The driveway lights caught the top of the driver and I could see he wasn't dressed for a Sunday night party in Beverly Hills. I stopped in the middle of the street and turned off my lights.

The guy in the Ford screeched off toward Sunset. I wasn't sure, but it looked like at least even money that Taylor was in the Ford. I started my car again and moved forward with the lights out. The Ford turned on Elm and I went after him, hitting the lights after I made the turn. If he kept running, I couldn't catch him, but if he kept driving this fast, chances were good the Beverly Hills cops would be around a bush and on his tail. He was two blocks ahead of me, crossing Carmelita, when he decided to slow down. When he made the left onto Santa Monica I was about a block behind him, feeling sure that, barring the long-feared attack of the Japanese Kamikaze fleet, I should be able to stay with him till I came up with a plan.

First, an admission. Being in the traffic on Santa Monica, following a killer with a gun, felt good, solid. No riddles, puzzles, goofy paintings, just a good, clean killer with a rifle. I was comfortable.

This was my town. These were the moments I lived for. I didn't even have to listen to the radio. I wished Gunther were there to share it, or Dash, or even Shelly. No, not Shelly.

Now all I needed was a plan.

7

wenty minutes later, the Ford pulled into a parking spot on Nicholas Street next to Lindberg Park, no more than twenty or thirty feet from where I had parked last night. I knew I had the right man and I knew where we were going—the house of Adam Place, the dead taxidermist. What I didn't know was why.

I kept driving and watched him through my rear-view mirror as he got out of the Ford, looked around, and crossed the street. I was in no big hurry now. I parked a block away and told myself to get to a phone and call the Culver City constables. I told myself, but I didn't listen. What did Alice in Wonderland say? "I always give myself such very good advice, but I very seldom follow it."

I got out, checked my .38, put it back in my holster and walked toward Place's place. There were no lights on in the house of stuffed animals, at least none I could see. No cop guarded the scene of the recent murder. Cops were too busy with wild sailors on leave and riots among the Mexicans. There was a red-on-white sign on the door: DO NOT ENTER. CRIME SCENE. BY ORDER OF THE LOS ANGELES POLICE DEPARTMENT AND THE CIRCUIT COURT OF LOS ANGELES.

I stayed away from the side of the house where Place's neighbor lived, the one who had called the cops the night before, but that cut down the possible entries. A good-sized fence blocked the view of the neighbor to the right of the house. I used the fence to cover me while I walked to what I was sure was Place's bedroom window.

There were no street lights in the neighborhood. Even if there had been, they would have been out by now. There was also no moon, because of a heavy cloud cover, which you'd never know by reading the papers—no weather reports were published or given on the radio for fear of aiding the Japanese in an attack. That never made much sense to me. The Japanese had to have better weathermen than we did in California.

I tried the window, but tried it so gently that I wasn't sure I was putting enough pressure on it even if it were opened and greased with oleomargarine. Someone, probably Jim Taylor, was inside the house with a rifle, and Jim Taylor had already taken a shot at Dali tonight, not to mention that he had probably shot both Claude Street in Mirador and Adam Place in the same bedroom I was trying to enter.

I pushed a little harder. The window was unlocked. It shot up with a rattle and there I stood, waiting for the bullet to go through my chest the way it had gone through the back of Dali's painting of Odelle. Nothing. I climbed in the window and tried to remember what the room looked like.

Then the light came on.

The man was about thirty or thirty-five, with a serious look on his face. His hair was movie star curly, and he looked a little like Gilbert Roland, except for the pock marks on his face. He wore a blue sweater, dark slacks, and a rifle aimed at my chest.

"Take out your gun with two fingers," he said.

"I can't take it out with two fingers."

"Take it out carefully."

I unzipped my windbreaker, showed my holster and took out my .38 very carefully.

"On the bed. Throw it on the bed."

I threw it on the bed. It didn't bounce.

"Now, close the window and pull down the shade," he said.

"I think—" I started.

"Close it now or I'll kill you."

His voice was vibrating like a cello string and he looked scared enough to mean what he was saying. I turned to the window, considered diving out, changed my mind and did what he told me.

"I opened it for you," he said as I turned to face him again. "The police locked everything. Cars are my living. I could have spotted your Crosley from the sound of the engine two blocks away."

"How did you get in?" I asked.

"Key. Adam Place was my cousin."

"Claude Street?"

"We got a mutual friend in Carmel."

"It doesn't pay to be related or friendly with you," I observed.

"I didn't kill them," said Taylor nervously. "Why should I kill them?"

"And you didn't shoot at Dali tonight?"

I took in the room without being too obvious about it, hoping there was something I could use, get to, someplace I could hide. The bed was there, still bloody. The bear was there, too. But the painting was gone. So was the clock. The rest of the room looked pretty much the way it had twenty-four hours ago, like a tidied-up version of Renfield's room in Castle Dracula.

"I shot at Dali," he admitted. "But not to kill him."

"Not to kill him."

"No, to get him to pay for the painting I still have, for the last clock. Don't you see? I got to get out of L.A."

"You want to run?"

"Someone killed Adam and Claude after they agreed to watch a clock and a painting for me. I have the last clock, the last painting. I want to give them back. That Dali's crazy. His wife's crazier. It was just supposed to be some kind of publicity thing, you know?"

"I know," I said.

"Hey, I just need a little money so I can get away. Police are gonna be after me. I know it and someone's killing— Look, I was gonna call, but you tell Dali. Tell him, tell her I need twenty-five thousand dollars and he can have his painting and his clock back. It's all their fault anyway."

"Their fault?"

"Stop doing that," he warned, pointing the gun in the general direction of my face.

"What?"

"Asking me questions. I'll tell you what you have to know. I wrote those messages on the paintings. It was Dali's idea, Dali and his wife. If they'd just have let me alone. We was doing all right."

"We?"

"Me, I. I like my work. Zeman treats me fine. I love cars. You love cars?"

"Adore them," I said.

"You're lying," he said, his voice rising. "I see what you're driving, how you don't take care of it."

"You're right," I said. "I hate the goddamn things."

When you talk to a nervous man with a gun, remember he is always right.

"Where was I?"

"Messages on the paintings," I reminded him.

"Yes," he said. "I wasn't supposed to take the clocks, the third painting. It was just a publicity stunt. I take the two paintings. They hire someone to look for them."

"Me."

"Yes, they hire you to look for them. I leave the messages and you get the paintings back. Then the newspapers come in. Maybe Lowell Thomas and Movietone. That's what they said. And I'd get a thousand dollars."

"Did Zeman know?"

"That," he said, "is a question. If you ask another question . . ."

"The clocks and the paintings," I reminded him, careful not to make the reminder a question.

"I needed help carrying the paintings. I drove to Carmel with Claude. When he saw the third painting and the three clocks, he was, I don't know, crazy. He told me we could make thousands and thousands."

I almost asked how, but caught myself and switched to, "Lot of money for a painting and some clocks. He must have thought they had some special value."

"Claude was smart. Claude knew about art, history, stuff like that. He could speak languages—Spanish, Russian, Dutch. I don't know anything about all that, painting, clocks," Taylor said. "I only know about—"

"—cars," I finished.

Taylor was shaking his head now. The finger on the trigger of the rifle was twitching nervously.

"I didn't kill anybody," he said.

"Gregory Novak," I tried.

"Gregory Novak. Who the hell is Gregory Novak?"

"Someone who might have killed Claude Street, maybe killed Adam Place, too."

"I don't know anybody named Gregory Novak," he

said. "I've got the last painting and the last clock. Dali wants them back, he gives you twenty-five grand by noon tomorrow."

"You mean tomorrow, Tuesday."

"Monday."

"Today's Monday. It's after midnight."

"Today. I'll call you at your office. You don't have the money, I don't know what I'll do. I'll kill Dali or I'll call the police, tell them about the whole thing, tell them it was Dali and his crazy wife's idea and they got Adam and Claude killed. I don't know what I'll do."

He was scared and ranting now.

"I'll let him know," I said as calmly as I could.

"The second clock's not here," he said. "I looked for it all through the house. Where is it?"

"Police probably took it."

"Why?" he asked. "Did they give it back to the Spanish loony?"

"They didn't tell me, Jim."

"Don't call me Jim. I'm not your servant."

"They didn't tell me, Mr. Taylor."

"Now you're making fun of me."

"What do you want me to call you, for Chrissake?" I asked.

The gun went off. Either he was serious about shooting me if I asked a question or the finger-twitching had worn down the trigger spring. The bullet tore past me into the wall and I turned and dived through the window, taking the shade with me. The shade kept me from getting cut by the shattering glass. I did a belly flop on the grass and lost my wind. I tried to get up but didn't have the air so I rolled to the right, pushing the torn window shade from me and expecting another shot from Taylor. He might not be able to shoot straight, but given enough chances at a close target he was bound to meet with some success eventually.

No shot came as I got to my knees, but I did hear Taylor coming out the window after me. Lights came on in the house on the other side of the fence as I heard Taylor move toward me in the darkness.

"Twenty-five thousand, cash, by noon," he said. "I'm a desperate man."

And I'm a weary one, I thought, but said nothing. I couldn't have said it even if I wanted to. I was still trying to get a near-normal breath. He moved past me, running toward his car across the street, the rifle in his right hand.

I hobbled in the general direction of the Crosley. There was no telling how long it would take the cops to show up; I'd guessed wrong about that the last time I was here. Taylor was down the street and long gone when I made it to my car and got in. There were no more lights on in the houses along the street, but I had the feeling people were watching from dark windows. They couldn't have missed the shot and the explosion of glass.

No police cars screeched around the corner ahead of me to cut off my escape and I saw none in the rear-view mirror. I should have gone back for my gun after Taylor had left. It was too late now. I headed for Beverly Hills, half shot near sunrise, in need of a shave, and trying to think.

I stopped at the all-night Victory Drugstore on La Cienega and got change from a woman of who-knows-what age behind the counter. She had a round pink face and a smile that said she was either simpleminded or believed fervently that Jesus was coming no later than Wednesday to take her out of this miserable job.

"Got coffee?" I asked her.

"Lunch counter's closed," she said. "But I can heat up what was left in the pot, if that's okay."

"That's fine," I said, heading for the phone in the back of the store.

My first call was to Zeman's. It was answered by Zeman himself.

"Did you call the police?" I asked.

"No," he said wearily. "The Dalis don't want the police involved. They think they'll be arrested. Dali's afraid of jails. He spent a few days in one in Spain when—"

"They can't stay with you," I said.

"They can't?" He brightened considerably.

"Your chauffeur may try to kill them," I explained.

"My . . . Taylor?"

"Taylor," I confirmed.

"Why?"

"Ask the Dalis. I'm sending someone to pick Gala up in the next hour, a big bald guy named Jeremy Butler. He'll take her back to Carmel and keep an eye on her. I don't think Taylor wants to hurt her, but let's not take chances."

"I can't believe J.T. would—"

"He shot at Dali. He tried to kill me about ten minutes ago. A second man named Gunther Wherthman will pick up Dali. You can't miss him. He's a little over three feet tall."

"Peters, did Dali put you up to this? Is this one of—"

"Barry, I'm getting them out of your house. You owe me a bonus."

"I said I'd pay if you got the . . . all right. Let's compromise. Five hundred dollars."

"Deal," I said.

"What if I can't talk them into going with your men?"

"Do your best. Tell them they'll stand a good chance of being dead by dawn if they don't. Tell them their only other choice is to go to the police. My men are already on the way."

"Where are you taking Dali?"

No answer from me.

"I see. You think I might be . . ."

"It's easier not to tell you and not to have to think about it, especially when you owe me five hundred bucks. One more thing."

The pink-faced night clerk came over to the open booth, bearing a white mug filled with steaming coffee. I nodded and took it gratefully. She looked pleased.

"What?"

"Taylor wants twenty-five thousand dollars by tomorrow to return the last clock and the last painting. Can you get it and give it to Gunther when he comes?"

I took a sip while he thought about it. The coffee was bitter, strong, with grounds at the bottom. It was just what I needed.

"Cash?"

"Cash."

"I can't believe Taylor . . . I've got that much in the house. I'll give it to your dwarf when he comes. I'll want a receipt."

"He's a little person, not a dwarf."

"I'm sorry," said Zeman. "I don't know the protocol. I know . . ."

". . . cars," I finished. This was deteriorating into the same conversation I'd had with Taylor. "Since you've got cash around, give the five hundred you owe me to Gunther in a separate envelope. Still think Salvador's a good investment?"

"Yes," he said. "You want to know what you should do with that five hundred?"

"What?"

"American Bantam. Out of business. Making Army vehicles now. You can pick up any one of the 1941 line for about three hundred. They'll be worth thousands in twenty years, maybe ten."

"Thanks." I hung up.

Then I called Jeremy. Alice answered.

"I woke you," I said, looking at my father's watch. It said it was nine, which was a lot closer than it usually got. I figured the time for two or three in the morning.

"No," she answered. "Jeremy was reading to me. He just finished a new poem. I'll get him."

I was down to the thick grounds at the bottom of the cup. The pink-faced clerk seemed to sense it and appeared next to me, gesturing with the tilt of an imaginary cup to her lips. I nodded yes and handed her the cup.

"Toby," said Jeremy. "I just finished a poem I'd like you to hear."

I was about to ask the man to leave his work, his wife, and his baby to drive a lunatic painter's wife to Carmel. The least I could do was listen to his poem. "Go ahead," I said. And he did:

> The filigreed fingernail of God
> etched a fine bright line across the sky
> as I watched through the window and heard
> behind me the patter of an insurance salesman.
> Over my shoulder I saw my wife nod,
> for she had seen the wonder, as I,
> had seen the heavenly bird
> over the patter of the insurance man.
> "Did you see that?" she asked him
> in joy. Eyes beclouded, dim,
> he answered, "It's nothing, let's insure your car.
> It's nothing, just a shooting star."

"I like it," I said.

"What did you feel?"

"Sorry for the insurance man," I said.

"Yes," said Jeremy. "Yes."

I told Jeremy what I needed. He listened, then asked if I really felt this was essential. I said it was and he agreed. I thanked him, hung up, and dialed Mrs. Plaut's, wondering if I felt sorry for the insurance man for the same reason Jeremy did.

Mr. Hill answered the phone and told me that he had to be up in two hours to get to the post office and sort his mail. I told him I was sorry, that it was an emergency.

"Nice New Year's party," he said.

"Nice party," I agreed, and he went to get Gunther.

"Toby?" asked Gunther in a voice coated with sleep.

"Gunther, I need a favor."

I explained and he readily agreed to pick Dali up and take him to my room.

"Gwen had to go back to San Francisco for a few days," he explained.

"Sorry," I said.

"Just a few days," he reminded me in his Swiss accent, which to too many people sounded suspiciously Germanic.

"I appreciate this, Gunther," I said.

"I have not always appreciated Señor Dali's insensitivities," he said, "but I am intrigued by his art. It should be most interesting."

"Thanks, Gunther," I said and hung up.

I had one more call to make, but I wanted to think about it for a few seconds. The counter woman came back with the second cup of coffee.

"Thanks," I said.

"Glad to," she said. "Slow at night. Most nights. I'd close it up but my son, it's his store. My husband and I take turns nights till Miles gets back from the war."

"Army?"

"Marines," she said with a big smile. I could see both pride and fear in it.

"It should be over soon," I said.

"Admiral Halsey, Bull Halsey, says we'll have the war won by 1943."

"He should know," I said.

"Commander of the South Pacific Force of the Pacific Fleet," she said. "He should know. Want something to eat?"

"I don't want you to . . ."

"I like the company," she said brightly.

"Got cereal?"

"Just Wheatena left."

"Sounds great."

As she bustled back to the lunch counter, I dropped my next nickel and called the Wilshire District Police Station. I didn't have to look up the number.

"Briggs?"

"Sergeant Briggs, right," came the Irish-accented voice.

"This is Toby Peters. Someone just stole my gun."

"Stole your gun," he said flatly. "You got a story to go with this? Some bullshit. Things are slow here and I could use a tale or two."

"Someone broke in my car, took it out of my glove compartment. I'm reporting it. I was parked on Santa Monica near La Cienega. Happened about four hours ago. I just noticed it when I went to lock it up at home."

"Maybe the Japs took it. Or those Fifth Col-youmnists."

"Could be. You want the serial number? I've got it right—"

"I'll get it off the records," he said. "But you've got to come in and fill out the papers. You know."

"Can it wait till morning, late?"

"Why not?" said Briggs. "I'll have the blotter report on your brother's desk when he comes in. He likes a good read with his first cup."

"Thanks, Briggs," I said and hung up.

My guess was that the .38 I'd thrown on Adam Place's bed was already on the desk of a cop in Culver City. I had the Wheatena and talked to the counter woman, whose name was Rose. I'd read her wrong. She wasn't simple and she wasn't waiting for Jesus. She was waiting for Miles Anthony McCullough, waiting for someone to show photographs of her grandchildren to. I ate my Wheatena and looked at the kids. They were all cute and they all looked like Rose McCullough.

8

The coffee kept me awake till I hit Mrs. Plaut's boarding house. I had trouble parking on Heliotrope, even with a car the size of my Crosley, but I managed to squeak into a space about two blocks away. The night light was on. I made it up to my room, kicked off my shoes, unzipped my windbreaker and placed it on one of my two kitchen chairs. My pants went on the other. My shirt had been through a tough day so, reluctant as I was, I retired it till I could find the time to wash it. My retired shirts made a small pile in the closet.

I checked the time on my Beech-Nut Gum wall clock and lay down on the mattress on the floor. I'd shave in the morning. I'd brush my teeth in the morning. I'd change my underwear in the morning. I'd become a better person in the morning. Right now I'd just lie there with the lights on and wait for Gunther to get back with Dali. That was my plan.

What was it the insurance man had said in Jeremy's

poem? "It's nothing, just a shooting star." I closed my eyes and saw the shooting star. Was I an insurance salesman or a poet at the window? I was asleep before I could think of an answer.

I dreamed of stone women crumbling in the sand, of mustaches without faces, of derby hats floating, eggs opening with something coming out that I didn't want to see, of Gala's clocks melting on Rose McCullough's grill at the Victory Drugstore. Koko the Clown kept popping up from behind rocks and through holes in screaming birds. He grinned but refused to play a major role in the dreams.

When I opened my eyes, Dash the cat was sitting on my chest and Gunther Wherthman, hair neatly trimmed, in three-piece suit complete with pocket watch and chain and black shoes polished to look like glass, was sitting on the sofa. He had a fat leather briefcase in his lap.

"You were asleep when we came in," he said.

I scratched Dash's head, eased him away, sat up and tried to rejoin the ranks of the living. It was no use. I lay back down and took a shot at focusing on Mrs. Plaut's pillow on the sofa, the pillow that had "God Bless Us Every One," neatly embroidered on it in red.

"I have fed the cat," Gunther said, handing me the briefcase and an envelope. I put the briefcase on the floor next to the bed, and tore off the end of the envelope. Five hundred-dollar bills drifted into my lap.

This held little interest for Gunther.

"Dali brought with him a rolled-up painting he says someone killed. It's in my room. Toby, I spoke to him in both French and Spanish and find difficulty understanding him in either."

"Where is he, Dali?" I asked.

"Downstairs, talking to Mrs. Plaut."

"Shit," I said, forcing myself up. "Where did he sleep?"

"He did not sleep. He says he takes little naps during the day. It gives him more dreams to work from."

"He can have some of mine," I said, looking around for my pants and, after several false starts, remembering they were draped over one of my two kitchen chairs. I shoved the five hundreds into a front pocket and struggled into the pants, while Gunther told me that Mrs. Plaut had invited us all to breakfast.

"That is why I had to wake you," Gunther explained. "She insisted that you be down for breakfast quickly."

I grabbed one of my not-too-frayed shirts from the closet and blundered my way out of the room and toward the bathroom, listening for voices and hearing none outside one inside my head I didn't want to hear.

"I'll be right down, Gunther," I said. "And thanks for—"

"No," he said as I leaned against the bathroom door. "I owe you much more than I am able to give. I am pleased that you continue to feel that you can both call upon and rely upon me in moments of crisis."

And that I could. Gunther went down the stairs and I moved to the mirror. I had saved Gunther's life once, a couple of years back. He'd been accused of murder and was close to going up for it. I had blundered into the real killer the way I'd just blundered into the bathroom, and Gunther and I had been friends and next door neighbors ever since. He had gotten me the room in Mrs. Plaut's and for that I was forever perplexed.

I shaved without committing suicide, brushed my teeth by borrowing some of Mr. Hill's Dr. Lyon's Tooth Powder, ran my fingers through my hair and put on my shirt. The face in the mirror looked presentable: nose flat, face baked by the sun, black-graying hair with gray sideburns a little long and in need of a cut. The movies didn't want me to star, but people sometimes needed someone who looked like me, sold his loyalty at a reasonable price, was willing to take a fall or two, could keep secrets large and small, and didn't give up on a client—although Dali had sorely tried me on that one. I went back to my room, grabbed the briefcase, checked the bills in my pocket, and hurried downstairs to find my client.

I got down to Mrs. Plaut's kitchen, just off of her sitting room. Gunther, Mrs. Plaut, and Dali looked up at me from the table. Mrs. Plaut was reading from her memoirs, which were stacked in front of her. Dali was dressed in a purple velvet suit and a black bow tie. Gunther looked happy to see me. In the sitting room, Mrs. Plaut's bird chirped insanely.

"Apples Eisenhower," said Mrs. Plaut, pointing to the dish of brown something in the middle of the table. "Since they were made with ingredients purchased with the aid of some of your ration coupons, I decided to overlook the fact that you did not return yesterday as you declared that you would."

"I was busy finding corpses," I said.

"It is delicious," said Dali seriously, wiping his mustaches.

I sat in the fourth chair and helped myself to a bowl of Apples Eisenhower and a cup of coffee. The Apples Eisenhower weren't bad, especially with cream supplied by Mrs. Plaut in a little blue porcelain pitcher.

Mrs. Plaut read from her memoirs, looking up from time to time for reaction from her honored guest. Dali listened intently and, when she caught his eyes, responded with an appreciative nod or an appropriate sound of approval.

Gunther and I ate and drank.

"Surrounded," read Mrs. Plaut. "No moon. No swords. No guns other than Uncle Wiley's Remington and the hand pistol Cousin Artemis had confiscated from the rebel soldier with the noticeable squint at Shiloh."

"Surrounded," Dali echoed. "Surrounded."

He liked the word.

"Surrounded," Mrs. Plaut agreed. "War cries and strange language came from the darkness. Aunt Althea began to pray and so did the woman named Mary Joan, who had joined them unbidden in St. Louis and who went on years later to marry a Sioux Indian named Victor or some such."

"Victor," said Dali, "an Indian named Victor?"

"Some such," said Mrs. Plaut, looking back at her manuscript.

I ate another bowl of Apples Eisenhower.

"Well," Mrs. Plaut went on. "It chanced that they were surrounded not by hostile Indians, but by some drunken members of the Pony Express who had wandered several hundred yards from their way station and were engaged in a jest. There was not much to do in way stations but drink, lie, and pester trekkers and Indians. The riders of the Pony Express were not the highest order of humanity, according to Uncle Wiley. One of them, not on the night of which I write, but on another much earlier, mistook or claimed to mistake Cousin Arthur Gamble for a buxom female and attempted to take liberties."

"Delightful," said Dali, beaming.

"Cousin Arthur Gamble on that occasion shot the Pony Express rider and was recruited to take his place on the morning run, which Cousin Arthur Gamble undertook."

"And this took place in . . . ?" asked Dali.

"Black Hills," said Mrs. Plaut, closing her manuscript.

"Señora Plaut, you are a true Surrealist," Dali declared, clasping his hands together as if in prayer.

"I am a Methodist," she answered, placing the manuscript to the side and reaching for the Apples Eisenhower.

"Amen," I said. "Sal, I think you should dress in something a little less gaudy. We're trying to keep a killer from finding you."

"The gaudier the crook, the cheaper the patter," said Mrs. Plaut, a spoonful of cream and apple near her mouth. "*The Maltese Falcon.*"

"This," said Dali, "is the most sedate costume that I possess."

"And the mustache," I went on. "It has to go."

"*Nunca*, never. I would rather die than lose my *bigotes.*"

"Well," I said cheerfully, "that may be one of your options."

"It's like family," said Mrs. Plaut, beaming. "My neighbor's brother back in Sioux Falls had a brother Beemer who had a mustache like Mr. Fala here. Beemer fancied himself a Mexican bandit, which was foolish since he looked not dissimilar from Grover Cleveland. Would anyone like some coffee?"

"Fala," said Gunther earnestly, "is the dog of the President of the United States."

I got up while I was still sane. "Sal, we've got to go."

Dali rose, took Mrs. Plaut's hand, and kissed it grandly. "You shall appear in my next painting."

Gunther got down from his chair, turned to me, and asked, "What do you wish me to do?"

"Nothing now, Gunther. I'll give you a call when I need you. Thanks."

As Dali moved toward the kitchen door and I followed him with the briefcase, Mrs. Plaut whispered loud enough to be heard across the Nevada state line, "If Mr. Fala is an exterminator, too, when does he have time to paint pictures?"

We didn't hear Gunther's answer. I got in front of Dali

and went to the front door. I checked the street through the window and then through the screen door. I didn't see any loony auto mechanics with rifles, but there were a lot of places to hide.

"Stay inside. I'm parked a few blocks away. When I pull up, come out and get into the car."

"I did not see all the grass when we arrived in the dark," he said as I opened the door.

"Well-trimmed," I said.

"Things lurk in the grass," he said softly.

"Stay on the sidewalk," I suggested, and went out on the porch and down the stairs.

When I got the Crosley turned around and back in front of Mrs. Plaut's, Dali made a velvet dash down the center of the sidewalk and into the street, where I had left the passenger-side door open. He jumped in, closed the door, and panted, holding his chest.

"It is bad. But not as bad at the Metro in Paris," he remarked.

I didn't follow up on that one.

We were downtown in ten minutes. On a good day when I was full of energy and had the time, I could walk from Mrs. Plaut's to my office. Since there had never been a good day that coincided with my being full of energy, I'd never walked to the Farraday Building. Normally, I parked at No-Neck Arnie's and filled the tank, if I had gas ration stamps, but it was a two-block walk from Arnie's and Dali stood out like a sore Surrealist. So I pulled into the alley behind the Farraday and parked in the Graveyard, a dirt plot where the bodies of three dead and rusted wrecks sheltered wandering winos.

I pulled in next to a frame that might once have been a DeSoto. Dali opened the door and stepped out. I slid over to the passenger seat with the briefcase and got out next to him.

"You live in a nightmare world," Dali said, looking around as a bum, who reminded me of a rotting pumpkin complete with an orange shirt, got out of the possible DeSoto and tried to focus on us. The bright sun didn't help much. Dali watched the man lurch toward us, pulling a pair of sunglasses from his pocket and perching them on his bulbous nose.

"What?" gargled the pumpkin.

"Two bits to watch my car," I said. "See nothing happens to it. No one touches it."

"Two bits?" the pumpkin asked Dali.

"No," said Dali, reaching into his pocket and coming out with crumpled bills. "Three dollars."

He held out the three bucks to the orange bum, who lifted his sunglasses and took the money.

"Anyone touches the car, he dies," the bum graveled. His gravel was even worse than his gargle.

"Come on, Sal," I said, moving to the rear door of the Farraday.

Dali followed, looking around the festering alley as if it were Oz. "It can get no better," he said.

"It can get a lot worse," I said. "My car could be gone by the time we come out. Our pal with the sunglasses isn't hanging around to watch my Crosley. As soon as we get inside the door, he'll take off for Erik's Bar. He's got enough money to keep him in Petrie wine for three weeks."

"Wrong," corrected Dali. "He will not depart when we go inside. He has already departed."

I looked back at Dali. He was triumphant.

"One can always count on man to find the deepest darkness of his soul."

"Comforting thought," I muttered, opening the back door of the Farraday with my key.

Dali went in ahead of me. "That smell," he said, his

voice echoing in the demi-darkness. "Perfume of nightmares."

"Lysol," I said, crossing the lobby.

"I have much to tell Gala," he said. "She will be in Carmel with your bald giant. I must call her."

"From my office," I said.

Dali admired the marble stairs and looked up the stairwell to the roof of the Farraday seven stories above. Voices came from behind doors. Off-key music. Some kind of machine. Something, maybe a baby, crying.

"Dante," he said.

"Let's go."

Dali got into the elevator and I turned on the third stair.

"You walk," he said. "Dali will ride upward into the Inferno."

"Sixth floor," I said and started up the stairs as Dali closed the cage door of the elevator and hit the button. I beat him to the sixth floor by about a week, even though the elevator hadn't stopped to pick anyone up or let them off.

"Magnificent nightmare," Dali said, joy in his voice.

"You ain't seen nothin' yet," I said, standing in front of the door to the offices of Minck and Peters. "Abandon hope all who enter here."

We went through the little waiting room and into Shelly's office. The great man himself was destroying the mouth of a man who lay still with his eyes closed. For his sake, I hoped he was dead. Shelly was probing with a corroded metal probe and singing "There'll Be a Hot Time in the Town of Berlin When the Yanks Go Marching In."

"Any calls, Shel?" I asked.

Shelly turned, shifted the cigar to the right side of his mouth, and replaced his thick glasses on the top of his nose by pushing the center of the right lens.

"No. Who's this?"

"Salvador Dali," I said.

"No shit?" Shelly turned to the dead man on the chair: "Mr. Shayne, this is Salvador Dali. He looks just like himself."

"Your studio is magnificent," complimented Dali, looking around at the sink full of instruments and coffee cups, the pile of bloody towels overflowing the basket in the corner, the cabinets covered with piles of dental magazines of a decade ago.

"I call it a surgery," said Shelly.

"You are an artist," said Dali. "America is mad."

Shelly beamed and nudged the dead man, who did not respond.

"I think you gave Mr. Shayne an overdose of gas," I said.

Shelly leaned over and put his head against the chest of the man in his tilted chair.

"He's alive. You trying to panic me, Toby?"

He moved away from Shayne and pointed his metal probe at the briefcase in my hand.

"What you got?"

"Twenty-five thousand dollars," I said.

"I don't need grief, Toby. I don't need jokes. I don't need grief. I need Mildred. Remember the receptionist I was going to hire?"

"I thought it was a dental assistant," I said, inching toward my office door.

"Whatever. Mildred objects. Jealous."

"I'm sorry, Shel."

"I'll live," he said, beaming at Dali. "Mr. Dali, you want a teeth cleaning? It's on the house. I'll get Shayne out of here for a half hour and—"

"I am not a *masoquista*," said Dali apologetically, "but I have friends in the motion picture business who would welcome your services. You have cards?"

Shelly stuck the probe in the pocket of his once-white smock and fished out a card. He handed it to Dali, who showed me the faint bloody thumbprint in the corner.

"Perfect," he said and followed me into my office. I closed the door and went behind the desk.

For some reason, I hoped he hated the closet.

"A tomb," he whispered, putting his right index finger to his lips and pointing with his left index finger at the photograph of my brother, my father, our dog Kaiser Wilhelm, and me when I was a kid.

"The dead," I said, sitting behind my desk and plopping the briefcase in front of me. "Guy in the middle's my old man. I know he's dead. So's the dog. My brother, the big one, is alive and a cop. You want some coffee?"

"I wish to call Gala," he said, sitting down across from me.

I pushed the phone toward him and pulled out my notebook to remind myself to bill him for the call.

After the twenty-minute call, in frantic French with Dali bouncing up and down, we sat looking at each other for about ten minutes.

"You play cards?" I asked.

"You have Tarot cards?"

"No."

"I do not play cards. You have paper, pencils?"

That I had. I fished into my top desk drawer, around frayed photographs of Phil's kids and pieces of things best forgotten, to find some crumpled sheets of typing paper. I also found a few pencils. I handed the package to Dali, who cleared away a space on the desk, looked at the wall, and said.

"Do not speak to Dali until he speaks to you."

"You got a deal. Mind if I use the phone?"

"Call—but do not, I say, do *not* talk to Dali."

It was nearly ten. I didn't want to tie up the phone too

long in case Taylor wanted to make his move early, if he was going to make any move at all.

I called Ruth, reminded her that I would pick up the kids after school on Wednesday, and asked how she was doing. She told me that surgery had been rescheduled for Wednesday morning.

"I could get Mrs. Dudnick to stay with the kids," she said. "And my sister would come from Chicago if I called her, but I'd rather wait till I was through the operation before I told my family. And Toby, the kids love you. They'll . . . I hate to ask, but I'll feel better if you're here. And Mrs. Dudnick's right next door."

"I'll be there, Ruth," I said. "First thing Wednesday morning, as long as it takes."

"Phil says you'd volunteer and then not show up. He says I should have Mrs. Dudnick ready."

"This time Phil's wrong about me. I'll be there."

"Thanks, Toby," she said.

"I'll talk to you, Ruth."

And then I hung up.

"Illness," Dali said without looking up from his drawing. "I can smell it, feel it in my fingers."

"I thought I wasn't supposed to talk to you."

"You are not, but Dali can talk if he must."

He stopped suddenly, put the pencil down and looked at me. There sat a man I had not seen before—his face aged, his mustaches wilted just a drop, and his voice down an octave as he spoke slowly.

"Mr. Peters, I am not jesting when I say the painting must be found, must be returned to me. Dali will be destroyed if the painting is seen by a critic, a gallery owner, a collector. Dali will be destroyed as surely as he will be destroyed if Taylor kills me as he has killed his accomplices."

"I'll find the painting," I said. "And no one's going to shoot you."

Then, suddenly, the Salvador Dali mask—eyes wide, hands dancing—was back on. He leaned forward to draw and the phone rang.

"Toby Peters, Confidential Inquiries."

"Peters?" asked Taylor.

"I just said that."

"You have the money?"

"I have the money."

Dali looked up when I mentioned the money. The tips of his mustaches tingled like the antennae of an ant trying to feel the wind.

"Cash?"

"No, war bonds. Taylor, name a place and a time."

"I'm nervous, Peters," he said. "Can you understand that?"

"You're looking for sympathy from me?"

"I just want you to under—"

"I asked a question, Taylor. Last night when I asked you a question you tried to turn me into confetti. Let's do business."

"It's ten-thirty," he said. "I'll give you one hour to get to Slip Number Four at the San Pedro shipyard."

"Have the clock and the painting," I instructed.

"Come alone," he said. "Or you don't see me."

I hung up. Dali was looking at me.

"Stay here," I said, picking up the briefcase. "Shelly will get you something to eat. What do you like to eat?"

"Sea urchins," he said, turning the piece of paper he had been drawing on so I could see it. It was a rough sketch of me dressed in a lace collar. It might be worth something someday. I opened the briefcase and eased it in so the bills would cushion it.

"Lovely," I said. "I'll be back in three hours. Stay in the office. If you need the toilet, Shelly will give you the key—it's down the hall across from the elevator. There's a radio in the bottom drawer of my desk. Don't answer the phone. Shelly will take care of it."

"You will get my painting?"

"I will get your painting," I reassured him, and went back into Shelly's office, closing the door to my cubbyhole behind me.

The man in the chair, Shayne, still looked dead. Shelly stood next to him reading a magazine and chomping on what was left of a cigar. He looked up at me.

"I'm waiting for the stuff to set," he explained. "Getting an impression for a bridge."

"Stuff? Is that what it's called?"

Shelly shrugged, dropped the magazine on the corpse's lap and said, "Tell me the truth, Toby. You think Dali needs dental work?"

"No," I said. "Don't even ask him. Keep him in my office and get him something to eat later."

"Please," he prompted, tilting his head back to keep his glasses from falling.

"Please," I said.

"The briefcase," Shelly said. "You don't really have . . . ?"

I opened the briefcase and tilted it so Shelly could see the bills.

"Twenty-five thousand," he sighed.

"Holy shit," exclaimed Mr. Shayne, miraculously resurrected by the sound of money.

Shelly turned to his patient. "That'll cost you another five bucks. You ruined my mold."

"I'm not paying," said Shayne, spitting out the chunk of pink gook.

My office door opened and Dali, paper in one hand, pencil in the other, watched doctor and patient shout at each other, their faces inches apart, Shelly's cigar dangerously close to Shayne's nose. Dali smiled at me and I left.

I could make San Pedro in forty minutes, Avalon to Anaheim, and then down Pacific. I could have made it in forty minutes. I could have, but I didn't.

The first problem was the pumpkin bum in the sunglasses. He was standing in front of my Crosley, arms folded, legs spread apart. Clutched in one of his fists was a rusted and slightly bent piece of metal that looked as if it had been ripped from one of the wrecks. His legs were a little wobbly, but he looked determined.

"You did a good job," I said, trying to reach past him to the passenger door.

"Don't touch the car," he warned.

"It's my car. Remember me? I offered you two bits."

"Other guy gave me a finif."

"I was with the other guy. He gave you three bucks."

"Yeah? What'd he look like?"

"A skinny little guy in a velvet suit with a pointed mustache a foot long."

"What else?" asked the rotting pumpkin.

"Get out of my way," I said.

I hadn't worked out in weeks and my leg wasn't back to subnormal. I didn't want to do battle with the demented of Los Angeles. It would be a life-long losing task, and time was ticking away. Besides, the guy was doing his job. There was honor in the alley—misplaced, confused, but honor. I didn't want to hit him and I sure as hell didn't want him to hit me with his corroded club.

"Let him pass," came a voice I recognized from above.

The pumpkin man took off his sunglasses and looked up. So did I. There, on the sixth floor, in the window of my office, Dali leaned forward, arms folded across his chest. Then his right hand came out and pointed upward. "Dali has spoken."

"What'd he say?" asked the pumpkin.

"He said, 'Dali has spoken.'"

The bum stepped out of the way. I opened the car

door, threw the briefcase on the floor, and scooted across to the driver's seat. The bum threw away the metal bar and leaned in the door.

"Is he, you know, one of Jesus's helpers? Like the elves and Santa Claus?"

"Yep," I said.

"I tried out for Santa Claus at Macy's," he said.

I motioned him back and leaned over to close the passenger side door. Through the window I could hear the bum say, "Least I wanted to, but you know something? I couldn't find Macy's."

Since I didn't have a working watch, the only way I could tell the time was turning on the radio or looking in store windows for clocks. When I'm late, I want to know the time, but I don't want to be told. It makes me nervous. So I try to find music. I could sing or think. I didn't feel like doing either.

I did a fair job of girl, clock, and people watching all the way to San Pedro. I parked a block away from Slip 4, got out, looked around for yet another clock, and hurried toward the shipyard.

There was a war on and there were ships being built. Beyond the gate about a hundred yards away giant cranes hovered over the hulls of massive Liberty ships, feeding them steel beams the way a bird feeds worms to its fat new babies. Flashes of fire and sparks from welder's arcs crackled over the decks.

Then there was the noise. A clattering of hundreds of air hammers, the growl of crane horns, the clang of flangers' mauls on bulkheads.

There were not only two guards in gray uniforms at the gates, but two armed Naval Shore Patrolmen with black holsters and serious personality problems. There was no other way in. When a guard looked my way, I walked right up to the gate.

One of the guards, who looked about twenty years

older than the forty he had looked like from across the street, stepped out to greet me.

"Can I help you?" he shouted.

"I'm late," I shouted back. "Car broke down a block away. Kelly in payroll's waiting for this."

I held up the briefcase.

"Kelly?"

"Kelly, Kennedy, some Irish name," I yelled with irritation.

"He means Connelly," came the second guard, moving to join us. The second guard was even older than the first.

"Connelly didn't leave any message about . . . What's your name?"

"Bruno, Bruno Podbialniak, First Security Bank of Hollywood," I said, reaching into my pocket for a business card. I really had one somewhere among the dozens of other cards I'd picked up over the years. When I had need of a bank or a banker, Bruno was it. I cost him more in cards than he and First Security made on investing my few bucks.

I knew where Bruno's cards were in the wallet, at the bottom of the pile in the bill compartment, right in front of one that read: "Kirk Woller, Mortician to the Stars." I handed a card to both guards who looked at them and then at each other.

"I'll give Connelly a call," said the second guard.

I looked at my father's watch impatiently. I was going with the punches. Don't think, I told myself. Just run the combinations.

The two Shore Patrolmen kept their distance but watched me carefully, their hands hooked into their belts very close to their holsters. The Shore Patrolmen were a good ten years younger than I had thought from across the street. One of them looked like my nephew Dave, only bigger. I watched the second guard go to a phone just inside the iron-mesh gate and make his call while the first guard read Bruno's card seven or eight times.

"One of my kids, Al's a banker," the first guard said. "Got four kids and a bad ear. Four-F."

I nodded and looked at my watch.

"Connelly wants to talk to you," the second guard called from the phone.

I strode through the gate past the teen Shore Patrolmen and took the phone from the guard.

"Connelly?" I said with irritation. "My car broke down and I've got other stops to make. Will you tell these people to take me to your office?"

"Who are you?" asked Connelly, who was a woman.

"Bruno Podbialniak. Your boss called and said to bring you this cash now. If you don't want to sign for it . . ."

"My boss? Monesco?"

"I guess," I said wearily. "Will you talk up. It's noisy out here. I'm late and I've got to get to Lockheed by four."

"Monesco isn't here today," she said. "He's—"

"Okay," I interrupted. "That's it. Porter can send someone else and you can tell your Monesco that—"

"Wait," said Connelly. "You have cash?"

"Cash."

"Show it to the guard who was on the phone."

I handed the phone to the guard and opened the briefcase to show him the bills. He shook his head and spoke to Connelly.

"Man has a lot of dollars," he said. "Okay." And then to me, "She wants you to give it to me and I'll give you a receipt."

"Forget it," I said, snapping the briefcase shut. "I was told to give it to Connelly personally and get a receipt. Besides, this is a twenty-dollar briefcase. I'm not donating it."

The guard got back on the phone and gave my story to Connelly. Then he listened, nodded, and hung up. "Says I should bring you over to payroll, Carl," he called. "I'm bringing Mr. . . . uh, the gentleman to payroll."

Carl nodded back and the two Shore Patrolmen examined me. I frowned at them. I was a busy man. I followed the old guard to a khaki coupe and got in. We drove past Slips 1, 2, 3, 4, and 5.

"What time you have?" I asked.

"Quarter to twelve," he said, pulling into a space next to a two-story building with aluminum sides.

I got out quickly.

"I know where it is," I said, slamming the door as he started to get out. "Wait for me here. It'll only take me a minute or two."

He shrugged and sat back behind the wheel and I hurried into the building with the briefcase. I pushed the door closed behind me and the world went silent. I didn't have time to enjoy it. I bypassed a time clock and a rack of cards and moved past an office with a little window. Inside the office, a man sat hitting the buttons on an adding machine. A sign on his desk, gold letters on a black background, said he was Arthur Mylicki.

I hurried down the hall looking in other rooms till I found an empty. I went in, picked up the phone and told the operator I wanted Arthur Mylicki's office. Two rings and Mylicki answered.

"Yes."

"Mylicki?" I coughed and continued in a hoarse voice. "This is Monesco. I've got a man with me from the bank. One of the guards is waiting for him outside your door." I coughed again.

"I heard you—"

"Damn cold," I said. "Had to come back. Payroll

problem. Tell the guard Connelly will bring Podbialniak back to the gate when we finish."

I hung up before he could say anything else and turned toward the door. A thin man wearing suspenders and a green visor walked in.

"Adding machine repair," I said. "I don't see anything wrong with your machine, Mr. Mylicki."

"You got the wrong office," the man said. "Mylicki's first door when you come in, to the left. Left of the door. Your right now when you go back."

"Sorry," I said and went out. Mylicki was just coming out of his office. He went outside and I moved to watch him through the thick glass pane in the door. He talked to the old guard in the car, who nodded and backed his coupe out. I stepped back and waited till Mylicki entered and then moved slowly past him to the door. I watched while the guard drove back toward the gate and then I opened the door.

When I stepped out something was different but I didn't know what. Then I figured it out. The noise was gone. Not completely gone, but very nearly. I must have been close to a major lunch break for at least one shift, which meant I was late, maybe too late, not to mention that I had probably broken state, national, and security laws. I tried not to think about what would happen if I got caught. I also tried not to think that if I had gotten this far, how far could a real spy get?

Slip 4 was empty. At least I didn't see any people. I did see a ship about the size of a department store decked out in flags and a big "400" in white letters. The ship, the *Koloa Victory*, was ready to be launched, probably within a day. On both sides of the slip were steel towers, about four stories high, with cranes on top. I moved toward the platform that had been set up for a christening.

I looked around. Nothing. Nobody. Somewhere,

maybe on the ship, maybe on the wooden scaffolding around it, a chain clanked against the deck or the hull. I stood there for a minute, maybe two, and figured Taylor had either set me up or had decided not to wait.

"You're late," came a voice from I-didn't-know-where.

"You picked a goddamn stupid place to meet," I said. "How did you get in here? And how did you expect me to get in?"

"The money in the briefcase?" he asked.

I was getting a fix on him now.

"Right here," I said. "The clock and the painting first."

"Put the briefcase down," he said.

I had him now, the tower on the left, high up near the crane.

"First the clock and the painting."

"I can shoot you and take it," he said.

"You can't shoot straight. You couldn't hit me at ten feet last night. You start shooting and I get under the tower and then head for the nearest guard."

Silence. At least no talking. The chain was still clanking somewhere and I could hear the crackle of a welder.

"I've got your gun," he said.

I looked up at the tower, into the sun, shielding my eyes with the briefcase. I saw a figure leaning over the top.

"Come up," he called.

It was up or out. I moved under the tower and found a ladder. It wasn't much of a ladder and it wasn't easy going up holding onto a briefcase full of money, but up I went. There was no reason for him to shoot me on the way. I would drop the money. I figured I was safe at least till I got to the top, and I was right. My arms were knots and my legs shaking when I reached the platform and pulled myself through the opening. There wasn't much room, maybe the size of a small boxing ring if you take away half the space for the crane.

"Good view from up here," he said.

We were about five feet apart. He sounded like Jim Taylor and looked like Jim Taylor, but he wasn't Taylor. The skin gave him away. No pock marks. He had what looked like my .38 in his right hand. He was wearing gray slacks, a gray shirt, a hard hat, and a smile I didn't believe for a second.

"You work here?"

"I work here. Put the briefcase down."

"You're Taylor's brother," I said, taking a step to my left and holding onto the none-too-sturdy pipe railing while I caught my breath.

"Put it down," he ordered.

I held the briefcase over the side of the tower.

"Clock and painting," I said. "I drop this and it's snowing bucks over the Cal Shipyard."

"You drop it and you dive after it," he said.

"I give it to you and maybe I'm dead. No—if I'm going, I'm not leaving the money up here."

"Son of a bitch," he said, looking at his watch. "Lunch whistle's gonna blow any second. Gonna be a few thousand people right down there with lunch boxes."

"Let's go down, get out of here and go where your brother has the clock and the painting," I suggested.

"Okay," he said. "You go first."

"Give me the gun."

"No! You nuts?"

"I'm not going to shoot you. I brought the money. I want the clock and the painting. Besides, it's my gun."

"No. I give you the gun and when we get to Jim, you take the clock and the painting and keep the money."

"It's a problem," I admitted, "but this wasn't my idea."

The whistle blew. Actually, a lot of whistles blew, which meant it was noon.

"Shit," said Taylor.

"How about this?" I suggested. "You go down. I wait

till you get to the bottom and the place is crawling with lunchers. Then you tell me where Jim is. You have plenty of time to call him, tell him I'm coming. He's got the rifle."

Taylor considered this.

"You're a smart-ass."

"Better a smart one than a dirty one."

"Jim told me you're a smart-ass. You know why I set this up? Because I'm smarter than Jim. I'm five minutes older and five times smarter."

"I can see that," I said.

He took a step toward me and I extended the arm with the briefcase farther over the railing. It didn't stop him. He shoved my revolver into my stomach.

"Give it," he said.

I swung the briefcase around and hit him in the head as I threw myself against the crane. His hard hat went flying over the side of the tower. He fired a shot that went wild, in the general direction of Jupiter. I hit him with the briefcase again, this time in the hand with my gun. I hit him hard. I hit him as if my life depended on it. I didn't like it up here.

He dropped the .38. It clattered behind me. I dropped the briefcase, turned my back on Taylor and went for the gun. I saw it, about five feet away, the barrel hanging over the edge of the platform. I went flat on the wooden deck and reached for the gun. Taylor jumped on my back. I don't know if he came knees or feet first. I lost my breath, what was left of it, and knew I had a good chance of being both sick and dead. He was crawling over me toward the gun. I reached out and pushed it over the edge. I didn't see it fall but I did hear someone below let out a yell and I heard a shot. The .38 had discharged when it hit the ground.

Taylor had to make a choice now. If he threw me over, there was no way he could get away with the briefcase.

I didn't know how many people were down there now, but I could hear voices and one in particular that said, "Up there. Hey, look at that."

Taylor grabbed the case. I rolled over as he started down the ladder. I got to my knees, threw up, felt a little better, eased over, and started slowly after him. He was in much better shape than I was now, and going down fast. I looked down and tried to shout. Nothing came out. I gulped and then gave out a dry yell.

"Stop that man! He's a spy!"

I didn't look down again. I climbed as fast as I could and almost bumped into Taylor, who had stopped about twenty feet from the ground, where a crowd of spy haters had congregated.

"He's lying," Taylor said. "I work here. My name's Taylor. Pipefitter. Section Twelve."

"Spy," I said. "I'm F.B.I."

Taylor looked up at me and I whispered to him, "We can still walk with that money. You want to deal?"

He gritted his teeth as he looked up at me, but he nodded.

"We're coming down," I said. "Give us room. He just surrendered."

Sounds of applause below as first Taylor and then I hit the ground.

"You want help with him?" a guy with a chow-chow face said.

"We'll be fine," I said, pushing Taylor ahead of me. "I've got some men waiting for us at the gate."

"Here's your gun," said a woman with a snood and incredible breasts. "I think it's broke."

"Thanks," I said, putting the .38 in my pocket.

It was more than broken. It was dead, but I didn't want to leave it here.

"Back to your lunches," I shouted. "He won't give me any trouble."

It took us about a minute to clear the crowd. A couple of people patted me on the back and one or two took a swing at Taylor.

"Where's your car?" I asked.

He didn't talk, but he did move to his left toward a line of cars across from Slip 3. I followed him to a black Ford. He got in; I put the briefcase in the back seat and rummaged around in the glove compartment. There was a greasy cloth behind some candy wrappers. I took it out, removed my windbreaker, threw it on the floor in the back, slumped over and covered my face with the cloth.

"Go to the gate. Tell them I poked my eye out on some machine and you're taking me to the hospital," I ordered. "Drive fast and make a sudden stop. Look scared, panicked."

"You're gonna lose more than an eye today," he said.

"I'm glad we're friends again," I said. "Drive and remember the full briefcase in the back."

He drove and it went just fine. Under the cloth I moaned, groaned, and screamed. I could tell from the voice of the guy who stopped us that it was the old guard who had driven me to Payroll.

"Go on, go on," he said. "I'll call and tell them you're coming."

Taylor pulled into the street, and I turned my head and watched us shoot past my Crosley.

All in all, I was having a good day.

9

Taylor drove up Western. We didn't talk. I didn't have a plan and I was sure he was working on one. Once I was wherever we were going, there wasn't much to keep him and his brother from taking the money and keeping the clock and the painting. Or, for that matter, from keeping everything and sending me back in the briefcase.

I didn't get much time to think about it. Taylor turned right when we hit Rosecrans and then a few blocks later he turned left. We were on a street of little once-white one-bedroom houses that probably looked tired the day they were finished. There wasn't much room between the houses but the community made up for it by letting the weeds grow tall and the jungle make a comeback.

A pair of old guys were sitting on a porch next to the house we pulled up in front of. One old guy was sloppy fat, wearing a blue shirt with the pocket torn not-quite-off. The guy he was talking to was thin, dressed in a suit and tie and sitting straight up with his hands in his lap and his eyes watching us get out of the car.

"Taylor," called the fat man.

Taylor jumped out of the Ford and waited for me to get out with the briefcase. He didn't bother to look at the fat old man.

"Guy here's been waiting for you," said the fat man, looking at the well-dressed thin one.

"I've got no time," Taylor said, moving toward the house we were parked next to.

We started through the veldt and the thin man came alive, jumping out of his chair and cutting through the underbrush to head us off. He just beat us to the door.

Up close he didn't look as old as he had from the street, but neither did he look as well-dressed. His jacket was rumpled. His pants were worse, and the collar of his white shirt was frayed. I didn't like his tie either.

"Mr. Taylor?" he said, looking at both of us and barring our way to the door.

"Him," I said, pointing at my buddy.

"James Taylor?" the thin man asked.

"John Taylor," Taylor corrected sullenly. "I've got no time. Out of the way."

The man didn't move.

"My name, Mr. Taylor, is Frank Buxton. I came in response to James Taylor's call. He said I should be at this address one hour ago, that he had a clock of unknown vintage he wished me to evaluate. I knocked at the door but there was no answer."

"Forget it," said Taylor, muscling past Buxton. "We changed our mind."

"Then," said the thin man, "you will still have to pay my fee for home and office estimates. Twenty dollars for the time I have wasted. Eighty cents for gasoline."

"Send me a bill," growled Taylor, putting his key in the door.

"Payment now would be preferable," said Buxton. "In fact it is essential."

Taylor had stepped into the darkness of the house but had left the door open for me. Buxton turned to follow him but I put a hand on his arm and said, "Hold it."

He stopped, turned, and waited while I reached into the briefcase and came out with a bill. It was a fifty. I handed it to Buxton. Taylor was back in the doorway.

"Get in here, Peters."

"I have no change," said Buxton, standing there with the bill in his hand.

"Keep it," I said. "What time did Taylor call you?"

"Get in the house, Peters," Taylor said threateningly.

"At nine this morning. Said it was urgent."

"Thanks," I said and followed Taylor inside.

He closed the door and I stood there waiting for my eyes to adjust to the light trickling in through the closed shades and half-drawn curtains of the living room.

"John," I said. "I think you and Jim were planning to be greedy. I think you and your brother were planning to take Dali's money and keep the clock."

"Only if the clock was worth a lot of money," he said, walking across the room and pulling back the drapes.

The room wasn't exactly washed in light now, but I could see a little better. A green sofa with wooden arms sat against one wall of the room. There were spots on the green, turning white from too many bodies and too much sweat. The once-dark wooden arms were scratched with dirty yellow lines. There were two other chairs in the room. One was red, a washed-out red that had given up trying to look like silk the night Taft took his first bath in the White House. The remaining chair was blue with embroidered tree leaves only slightly darker than the background. There were two lamps, one on an end table between the chairs and one floor lamp trying to be modern but missing it by two decades. Newspapers were open and everywhere.

"Charming place you have here," I ventured.

"Jim and I haven't touched it since Mom died," he said, moving across the room to an open door. "Jim," he called.

I followed him. We looked through the bedroom door at two beds, twin beds that looked a bit small for the Taylor kids.

"Nice beds," I said, following him back into the living room.

"Mom and Dad bought them for us when we were seven. Where the hell is Jim? He was supposed to be here."

There was only one room left, the kitchen, where we found Jim seated at a square table with chrome legs and a white Formica top. Jim was face-down on the newspaper spread out on the table. I knew he was dead because something with a wooden handle was buried in the back of his neck. It was buried so deep that I couldn't see any of the blade. On the table, facing the handle, was a clock, the triplet of the two I had seen sitting in front of two other corpses over the past two days. This one wasn't ticking. The key was in the hole under the minute hand.

There was no painting. We'd taken the nickel tour of the place and I hadn't seen it. John Taylor stood, feet slightly apart, hands at his side, looking at his dead mirror image on the table.

"Go in the other room and sit down," I said.

Taylor didn't seem to hear.

"Go sit."

He was shaking now, like a little balsa wood model of a Spitfire. Like the one my nephew Nat had hanging over his bed.

"You're too big for me to carry, Taylor. Go sit down."

"You don't understand," he said, his face white.

"I've got a brother," I said.

"You don't understand. I hated him," said Taylor. "We were never him and me. We were us. No one thought about us as . . . as . . ."

"Individuals."

"Individuals," he repeated, his eyes fixed on his brother. "I hated him. I don't think I can live without him. I don't know how."

I wanted to tell him to save it for a headshrinker or his neighborhood priest, but he wasn't really talking to me. I moved to the table and touched the corpse. Still warm. I heard a sound and looked up at the window in the back door. Frank Buxton, the clock appraiser, was standing there watching. He blinked once and backed away.

"I think you can expect the police in about five minutes," I said, turning back to Taylor, who hadn't moved and didn't seem to hear.

"The police," he repeated dumbly.

"You know where the painting is?"

He shook his head no.

"You see the painting?"

He shook his head yes and said, "You want a liverwurst sandwich? That's all we . . ." His voice trailed off.

There was a large glass fruit bowl on the counter near the sink next to an open box of Kellogg's Pep. There was one rotting banana in the bowl. I took it out and put it in the sink. Then I opened the briefcase and shoveled about half the money into the bowl.

"That's for the clock," I said.

Taylor pulled his eyes from his brother and looked at the bowl of money.

"For the clock," I repeated.

"You're a straight shooter, Peters," he said.

"Like Tennessee Jed," I agreed.

"Sorry I tried to kill you."

I picked up the clock. It was damned heavy. It would have been bad enough if I weren't carrying the briefcase.

"Open the door," I said, "and get to a phone. Call the cops. You might beat Buxton to it. At least you'll be on record as having called."

He shuffled to the back door and opened it.

"And hide the money."

But John Taylor wasn't listening to me. He had turned his back to the door and stood facing his dead brother. I kicked the door closed and tried to keep from breaking my neck as I made my way down a narrow cement pathway to a dirt alley behind the house. The alley led to a dead end. I crossed a tiny yard with a lawn that had been mowed within the decade and found myself on a small street that looked just like the one the Taylor brothers lived on. I was sweating now and the clock was getting heavier. I lurched on like Lon Chaney in his mummy suit until I came to a street that showed some sign of life and led back to Rosecrans. I was about four blocks from the Taylor house now. Traffic was light in the early afternoon, but I spotted a Black and White cab and waved him down, balancing the clock and the briefcase in one hand.

"Nice clock," said the cabbie through his window.

"Thanks," I said and told him to head back to the shipyard.

I got my Crosley with no problem. The clock sat on the seat next to me and looked straight ahead all the way back downtown and into No-Neck Arnie's garage. I didn't even bother to look for a space on Hoover or Main and I wasn't going up against the pumpkin man again. I slid over, taking the clock in my arms, and got out. I reached back inside and retrieved the briefcase. I wasn't looking forward to carrying them both to the Farraday, but I sure as hell wasn't going to leave them with No-Neck Arnie.

"Peters," said Arnie, an overalled little man with a barrel chest and enough oil and grease on his body to fuel Huntington Beach for a week.

"Arnie," I said. "Fix the door."

"Busy," he said. "Where'd you get the clock?"

"Other side of hell," I said. "I'll be in my office about an hour. What'll it cost to fix the door?"

Arnie walked around to the driver's side door, wiped his hands on his overalls and tried to open it.

"You did that last week," I reminded him.

"Warp, heat, alignment differentials change in a week," he answered, in the mysterious tongue of auto mechanics.

"How much?"

"Twenty bucks," he said.

The clock was heavy, the briefcase handle sweaty.

"Twenty bucks," I agreed.

Arnie looked at me suspiciously.

"Twenty bucks," I repeated.

"I'll throw in a paint job," he said.

"You are a saint."

"I just like my work," he said. "Still can't do it till Thursday. You need another door."

"All right. Where's Syd?" I asked. Syd was Arnie's day assistant, a one-eyed guy with a bad stutter.

"Army," said Arnie, standing back to survey my Crosley.

"They let Syd join the Army?"

"Drafted," said Arnie, arms folded, deep in thought as he contemplated his task.

It took me a couple of months to get to the Farraday Building. People admired the clock along the way. Even had an offer to buy it. Twenty bucks. I trudged on and made it to the elevator around five o'clock. I almost fell asleep on the way up. A trickle of people came out of offices and made their way down the stairs, their footsteps echoing as they passed me, rising slowly in the groaning cage.

When I made it through the door to the office and into Shelly's house of pain, I found Dali in the chair, mouth open and Shelly hovering over him.

"Hold it," I said.

Shelly held it and turned to me.

"What?"

"Keep your fingers out of my client's mouth."

"My fingers aren't in his mouth. He—"

"I told him to look down my throat into eternity," said Dali, getting out of the chair. "If he can see eternity down my throat, then each time a patient sits here before him, Dr. Shelodon Minik can understand infinity, can sense forever. He will not be fixing teeth. He will be drawn into the creative vortex."

His wide eyes turned to me and my burden.

"Gala's clock. My painting?"

"Taylor's dead."

"And my painting?"

"I didn't see anything in your throat but tonsils," said Shelly.

"It cost half of the money. I got the clock and the guy who threatened to kill you is dead." I didn't see any point in mentioning Taylor's brother.

"I've looked down maybe a hundred thousand throats," muttered Shelly. "Saw double tonsils once or twice and—"

"Shelly," I said. "Take this."

I handed him the clock.

"It has never been wound," said Dali. "Legend says that it should only be wound at midnight or noon. The Russians have no imagination, only gross feelings."

"Your wife is Russian," I reminded him.

"Gala is the eternal. The eternal is Gala," said Dali, advancing on me, his voice dropping with each step and the name "Gala" coming out like a quiet "Amen."

"Anybody call?" I asked.

Shelly cradled the clock and started fiddling with the key.

"Leave it alone, Shel," I said. "Anybody call?"

"Jeremy. He says they're in Carmel. I lost him while he was talking. I think the phones are really out now."

"Anybody else?"

"The cop, Seidman," said Shelly, tilting the clock over and looking at the words in Russian printed on the bottom. "He said to tell you when you show up to come in and see him fast. About a dead guy named Taylor."

"Sal, we'd better get going. Shel, you haven't seen me."

Briefcase in hand I opened the door to the waiting room. Dali looked back and said to Shelly, "Perhaps it is better that you do not gaze too deeply into the darkness of man. Eternity is too frightening for some and too blissful for others."

"Remember my smiling tooth," said Shelly.

"I shall paint you a smiling tooth," said Dali gallantly.

"Make it look like that guy who paints for the *Saturday Evening Post*. Norman Rockwell. Now, he's a great painter."

Dali closed his eyes, breathed deeply. "I will consider it. Now we must get to Carmel. Tomorrow is the party."

I had Shelly carry the clock down to the front of the Farraday and wait while I went back to Arnie's and got the car. About ten minutes later, the clock between Dali's legs and the briefcase under his feet, we were on the way to Carmel. We didn't say anything for fifty miles and then Dali exploded.

"If you do not recover my painting, I shall swallow cups of paint till I die. I will become paint. I will pour it in my eyes, my ears, so I don't see or hear the taunting."

"You want to listen to the radio?" I asked.

"Yes, please," he said softly and with great calm. "I believe we can still hear Snooks."

Dali smiled through the show and nodded his head. Twice he looked at me when Baby Snooks said something that didn't strike me as particularly important. Dali's raised eyebrow suggested some profound depth to the statements: "But Daddy, Robespierre always eats bread and butter," and "Robespierre, don't sit on Mr. Goodwin's hat."

When the show was over, Dali looked out the window, asked, "What is the worst trip you ever took? In your life?"

I've been on some bad trips in my life. I told him about the time my father took me and my brother Phil to Lincoln, Nebraska, to visit his sister. I was five or six. We went on a train and had to sleep sitting up. I sat across from a woman in a black dress who took up two seats and kept eating little things she pulled out of her knitting bag. She smiled and offered me one. I was sure it was alive. I dozed off a few times but kept opening my eyes. Each time I did I found her looking at me, smiling and munching.

"Trains," said Dali. *"Ferrocarril.* I know. You must come hours early, tie each bag to your body with a strong string when you get on so no one will steal them."

"I'll remember that," I said.

"And sit as near the engine as you can so you will arrive earlier."

"Makes sense to me."

Dali told me about his worst trip in an automobile, ten years earlier, when he and his wife fled Spain. He was visiting his father in some place called Catalonia when the district declared its independence from Spain. Dali was convinced the civil war broke out because he had just spoken to his father after years and the gods were punishing him for his mistake. Gala had to find safe-conduct passes and a car to drive them to the French border through drunks and machine guns.

"I can still see the little village where we stopped for gasoline," he said, looking out the window. "The men are carrying ridiculous but lethal weapons, while under a big tent people are dancing to the *Blue Danube*. Then I hear four men talking about our luggage. One of them looks me in the eye and says I should be shot. I fall back in my car seat."

And with this Dali fell back, shaking the Crosley almost enough to drive us off the road.

"I gasp for breath," Dali said, gasping for breath. "My little cock shrivels like a tiny earthworm about to enter the mouth of a great fish. Our driver shouts filth and orders the men to get out of our way."

Dali went silent for a few miles, his eyes closed. I thought he had dozed off, but he suddenly said, "The driver got us to a small hotel in Cerbere, on the border. We found out later that as he was driving home, just outside of Barcelona, he was shattered by machine guns. It was the trap of that awful stupidity, civil war."

"Hungry?" I asked.

"Androgynous," he answered.

I didn't ask him what he meant. I figured he was making up a word. I looked it up later.

10

We took Highway 1, stopped at San Luis Obispo for coffee. Dali wouldn't leave the car. He got out clinging to the clock so I could slide out, and then he jumped back in the car, closing the door behind him as I ran into a place called Little Al's and Big Mary's Diner. I brought the coffee out along with three hot dogs, one with mustard, two with ketchup, all with onions.

"Hot dogs," said Dali, looking at the one with mustard, "are obscene."

He ate it obscenely and washed it down with coffee.

"When I came to this country I had the ship's baker make a baguette three yards long," he recalled excitedly. "What I should have had the cook make was a hot dog three yards long."

I was on my second dog and losing my appetite.

"Yes," he said, sitting back and finishing his coffee, "an enormous, obscene hot dog."

Then, suddenly, the excitement was gone, and he

whispered softly, "Find my painting, Toby Peters. Find my painting."

Several miles farther along I pointed out the road to San Simeon, but he wasn't interested. Since it was dark, there wasn't much to see and not much traffic. Dali closed his eyes and I listened to a band playing live on an all-night Fresno radio station. Over the music I could hear the surf along the beaches except when we passed through Lucia and Big Sur, where the hills blocked the sound. We hit Carmel just before midnight. I touched Dali's shoulder.

Without opening his eyes he gave directions to the house and added, "If one does not shave, one turns into an animal that soils his pants."

"I'll remember that," I said, driving down the road toward the sea.

The house was smaller than I expected, but I could tell from the noise of the ocean nearby that in the morning when the sun came up the view would be better than I had imagined.

A light was on.

"Do not park in the back," Dali directed.

"I don't want anyone to see my car from the road."

"Let me off at the door and then go to the back," he said, then turned to me and whispered, "Here there are . . . grazhoppers."

With that explained, I drove to the front of the house and slid out after him, reaching back for the clock and the briefcase. He hurried, being careful to stay on the stone path. The door opened before we could knock and there stood Gala and the massive figure of Jeremy Butler.

"Salvador Dali is here," said Dali.

"Salvador Dali is here," Gala repeated, taking his arm and touching his face to see if he had a temperature.

"There is a giant behind you." Dali pointed at Jeremy. "This is Jeremy," said Gala. "A poet."

Then she saw what I was carrying and sighed with relief. "Put him inside. I'll welcome him later."

We went in and Dali said, "This is a night of Lord Byron; he is the poet of this night. Terrors, creatures with tentacles all around us, and no comfort of the moon. I will not make such a voyage again without Gala."

"Escargot," Gala said comfortingly. "Snails with butter and garlic. Come." She led Dali away by the hand.

"Thanks for coming, Jeremy. Everything all right?" I asked, passing off the clock before I dropped it.

"Yes," he said, taking the heavy clock in one hand. "I read her some of my poetry, but she hears only one voice, that of Dali. She is very concerned that the costume party they are planning for tomorrow will be a failure and Dali will be ridiculed by the press."

"Is there a place for us to sleep here?"

"Bedroom, downstairs. Two beds. Dali's bedroom is upstairs."

Jeremy led me into a small but comfortable living room with thick, soft furniture. There were three paintings on the wall with their backs turned to us.

"Picasso's," Jeremy explained, putting the clock on a small table near the window. "Do you expect us to be here long?"

"Can't say," I said, sitting in one of the chairs and sinking in. "Three people are dead because of the missing painting and three clocks. Dali thinks the killer's dead. I think he's got Dali's painting and may not be too happy with Salvador."

"Do you have any . . . ?"

"I think his name is Gregory Novak, but beats the hell out of me where to find him."

"I will call Alice and tell her that I may be delayed."

"I'm sorry, Jeremy." I walked to the wall and pulled the first Picasso out so I could take a look at it.

"Alice is an admirer of Dali's work. She'll understand."

The Picasso painting, what I could see of it, since I didn't want to take it down from the wall, was a blue and yellow eye on a sea of something that looked like little question marks without the dots under them.

"Jeremy, what the hell does this stuff mean?"

"It means nothing," said Dali, coming into the room. "Nothing and everything. Picasso is a fraud. Dali's work escapes, goes beyond meaning into the eternal and mysterious unconscious. My Gala tells me you are a poet. Is what I have said not true of all art?"

Dali had changed quickly and shaved. He wore a tiger-skin robe from beneath which peeked the collar and the pants legs of pink silk pajamas. In his right hand was a glass with a stem about a foot long. The liquid in the glass was orange.

I let the Picasso drop back against the wall. Jeremy mused aloud: "Each artist, with rare exceptions, is his own Cassandra, doomed to tell himself the truth and doomed never to understand it. Surrealists say that their work has no meaning. The truth is that they are incapable of seeing what it means, and certainly they are incapable of saying what it means."

Dali had been sipping his orange drink when Jeremy began, but stopped almost immediately and then looked at Jeremy without expression.

"And who shall tell us what it means?" he asked softly.

"There are many who will tell you, but each has his own key—the Freudian, the Jungian, the Catholic, the Jew, the Marxist. Each has a key to the enigma we create and each is right yet each is only partly right because we ourselves are the only ones who can comprehend the meaning of our work, without words, if we will just look at it."

"And why do we not look at it?" asked Dali.

"Because we are afraid of what we will see," answered Jeremy. "Sometimes I think artists create so that others may see and the artist need not look."

"You are a romantic," exclaimed Dali, holding his glass up to toast Jeremy.

I didn't know what the hell they were talking about, so I said, "I don't know what the hell you're talking about and I need some sleep."

"Tomorrow we shall be busy," Dali announced. He placed his now-empty glass on a wooden table with a little round platform. The glass just barely fit. "Tomorrow is the celebration of the setting sun, and we shall all be in pagan costume to welcome the first devil's night of the new year."

With that, Dali raised his eyebrows and opened his eyes wide. His mustaches twitching, he turned and disappeared into the hallway.

"Where's the kitchen?" I asked.

"I'll show you," said Jeremy.

There wasn't much in the refrigerator that appealed to us after we finished the chilled shrimp and each had a large helping of orange juice in mugs shaped like babies' heads. Jeremy led me to the bedroom after we made the rounds and were sure the house was secure. Locked doors and windows wouldn't keep a killer out, but they would probably make it a little noisy to break in. We agreed to sleep in shifts, three hours each. Jeremy said he had some reading and wanted to stay up first, pointing out that I looked too tired to take the first shift. He was right.

There were two beds in the guest room. I washed my face, brushed my teeth with my finger and some Dr. Lyon's tooth powder Jeremy let me use, took all the stuff out of my pockets and put it on the low dark dresser against the wall, and then took off my clothes and hung them in the closet. Jeremy, fully clothed, sat on one of the beds reading.

"What're you reading?"

"Theodore Spencer," said Jeremy, "Listen:

> *The pulse that stirs the mind,*
> *The mind that urges bone,*
> *Move to the same wind*
> *That blows over stone.*"

"Sounds nice," I said, scratching my thigh through my underwear.

"I'll read it to Alice tomorrow," he said. "It's part of a longer work. If you like, I'll go in the other room to read."

"Don't bother. I'll be asleep in a minute. My problem's not getting to sleep, it's staying there."

And I was right. All I had to do was close my eyes and try to make sense out of what had happened in the last three days. I thought about Gregory Novak. I might even have said the name, but that was about all I did think or say before I fell asleep.

I dreamed of Gala in the kitchen singing "The World Is Mine Tonight" and making flapjacks on the griddle. She was wearing a frilly apron and doing her best to look like Betty Crocker. I was waiting for the flapjacks when Dali came in wearing overalls, a plaid shirt, and a straw hat.

"They're almost ready to harvest," he said, sitting at the table and grinning at me. He pointed to the window.

I got up and looked over the shoulder of the busy, singing Gala. The sun was white bright but I could see the shore—along the beach, in the sand, clocks were in bloom, black clocks just like the one in the other room. Music was coming from inside the house, dark music.

"Blood makes them grow," Dali said behind me.

And now I could see that the sand around each clock was red.

I woke up. Jeremy was sitting in the same position, still reading, but he was at the end of the book.

"Time is it?" I asked blearily.

"Four-thirty," he said. "I've checked the doors twice. I wasn't sleepy."

"I'm up now." I sat up. "Get some sleep."

I was awake but I could still hear the dark music.

"What is that?"

"Bach," said Jeremy. "A fugue for organ. I think Dali uses it for background music while he paints."

"Why not?" I got out of bed and almost crashed into the wall when my leg refused to hold my weight. I managed to steady myself by grabbing hold of the headboard.

"Would you like the book?" asked Jeremy.

"No, thanks," I said, making it to the closet. "I'm going to see if I can find some coffee."

Jeremy took off his shoes, removed his clothes, and put on a pair of clean pajamas that had been folded neatly in the small suitcase he had brought.

"Wake me no later than nine," he instructed, lying back and closing his eyes.

"We'll see how it goes," I said, slipping on my shoes. "You can turn off the light."

And he did.

I made my way into the kitchen. It was empty but I could still hear the organ. In fact, it made the floor reverberate under my feet. I didn't find coffee or cereal. There was a loaf of bread. I went into an enclosed deck on the sea-side of the house, opened the window so I could hear the surf, and sat in a straightbacked chair with the bread and glass of water. The sun rose somewhere over the Rockies and hit the shore. The view was great. We were on a ridge about fifty yards from the beach. The weeds were below the ridge and a sandy path led down just outside the window. Gulls swooped and sat on something near the shore that looked like a big chair.

"It's a throne," said Dali, looming up behind me. "I shall tell my guests tonight that it is the throne of Cleopatra's father."

I jumped up, my heart beating like a combination by Henry Armstrong.

"You scared the shit out of me," I remonstrated.

"It is the fate of man since clothing was invented to embarrass us that we should soil ourselves," he said. "In fear, in passion, in disgrace. It is a concern that only humans have, particularly fathers."

Dali was wearing the same tiger-skin robe and pink silk pajamas. He had one of those long-stemmed glasses in each hand. He handed me one.

"Orange juice," he said. "From my cache of fruit."

I took it and drank.

"Good stuff," I said.

"Today we find my stolen painting," he affirmed.

"Could be," I hedged.

"I saw it in a dream," he said.

"When did you sleep?"

"Here, there, a moment, an interrupted dream. I do not need light to paint. The light is in here."

He pointed to his head.

"Like a Mazda bulb," I said.

"Precisely. The Impressionists need light from outside, from nature, from the gods. Surrealists get light from inside themselves. They need no gods."

"Pretty weighty stuff for dawn," I said. "This is more Jeremy's line. Mind if I use the phone?"

"It is not chilled," he complained. "There is a phone

in the kitchen but I cannot bear to touch it. It sticks to the fingers. Phones should be chilled."

"I'll try not to be too disgusted," I said.

It was almost six on a Monday morning. I called the boarding house, hoping for Gunther. I got Mrs. Plaut on the second ring.

Before I could say anything, she shouted, "Early, but I don't care. I had to feed the bird."

"Mrs. Plaut, it's me, Toby Peters. Can you get Gunth—?"

"Mr. Peelers, the police are an interesting lot, Lord knows, but they spend entirely too much time here looking for you."

"The police were there?"

"Have you been killing people again, Mr. Peelers? I have asked you to stop that manner of behavior."

"I've never killed anyone, Mrs. Plaut," I objected. "Can I please speak to—"

"They asked me about a clock," Mrs. Plaut went on. "I showed them the Beech-Nut clock on the wall of your room, the grandmother clock in my sitting room, but they were not interested."

Dali was now standing in the doorway to the kitchen, empty glass in hand.

"Gunther Wherthman," I said loudly, emphatically, to Mrs. Plaut, to no avail.

"They talked to Mr. Gunther Wherthman also," she said. "I informed them that if they wanted to apprehend you for murdering more people they would be well advised to go search for you instead of indulging in hobbies."

"Allow me," said Dali, reaching for the phone.

He had a clean new handkerchief in his hand and took the phone carefully, like a hot-shot evidence man at a crime scene.

"*Señora* Plaut?" he asked into the phone. And then he

began to jabber away in Spanish, with appropriate pauses to listen. Finally, he said, *"Esta bien, gracias."*

He handed the phone to me and cleaned his hands.

"She's getting your Mr. Wherthman," he said. "I must dry my hands."

"Mrs. Plaut can't speak Spanish," I said as he threw into the corner the offending handkerchief that had touched an unchilled phone.

"Her Spanish is flawless," said Dali. "A bit of the Andalusian but perfect."

And he was gone.

"Toby?" came Gunther's voice over the phone.

"I'm here, Gunther."

"Police were here. Sergeant Seidman."

"Did they see the painting?"

"No, it is in my room, under the bed. They would not say why they were looking for you."

"Fleeing the scene of the crime, absconding with evidence, possibly suspicion of murder."

"That is less serious than last time," he said. "They wish you to come see them immediately. I believe that a police automobile with a red-haired man inside is waiting across the street."

"Thanks, Gunther," I said. "Here's my number. Don't write it anywhere."

"Be cautious, Toby," he counseled.

"I will," I said. "Did you know Mrs. Plaut speaks Andalusian Spanish?"

"Yes," he said. "And a very acceptable French."

"Why didn't I know that?"

"Toby, you are my closest friend, the closest friend I have ever had and yet you have an inclination to close yourself off from that which will alter your perception of others. Mrs. Plaut is an enigma, not a joke."

"I hate art and philosophy, Gunther. And I don't care all that much for literature."

"I know that you believe that, Toby. Please, I did not intend to agitate you."

"I'm sorry, Gunther. I don't really hate art and literature."

"I know that. Did you get enough sleep last night?"

At that instant, Gala, a twig in a purple dress reaching to the floor, washed into the room.

"No," I said.

"Off the phone," Gala ordered.

I turned my back on her. I had been about to end the conversation, but now I was more than a little inclined to engage Gunther in discussion of Da Vinci, Debussy, or Frankie Sinkwich.

"Recommend some reading for me, Gunther," I said.

"I have a party to arrange for Dali and only twelve hours to complete it," Gala said. "The phone is required."

"I will gladly make a list and let you borrow my books," said Gunther, "but I would prefer that you not remove them from Mrs. Plaut's premises."

"I'll talk to you, Gunther," I said.

"Be more concerned for your safety," he answered, and I hung up.

Gala took the phone from me and motioned for me to get out of the way and out of the kitchen. I left.

The rest of the day, Jeremy—after I woke him at nine—and I took turns watching the street. A couple of truckloads of caterers arrived around three and took over most of the house. The caterers were all women.

"This," declared Dali, who had changed into a white tuxedo with black tie and had come down to tilt his head back and watch the preparation, "must be a night of triumph. The press of the world will be here and I shall find new ways to offend."

"Sounds like fun for all," I said.

"I must retire to my rooms now." Dali refused to

acknowledge my sarcasm. "It is fatiguing to watch people work and to create offenses."

At five, with food everywhere and tables on the beach around the throne, the first guests arrived. No one came to the house. Dali had painted a sign that Gala had personally put up in the sand. The sign read:

TO THE BEACH FOR SIGHTS DENIED MOST MORTALS

These first guests, a man and a woman, were wearing clown costumes.

From the window, Dali observed to me, "No imagination. I shall be dressed from the neck down as a rabbit—a trickster who hops, deceives, and refuses to be contained. And from the neck up, I shall be Sherlock Holmes, who claims to operate from reason and the logic but is really an artist."

"Have fun," I said.

"And you shall be dressed as . . . ?" Dali inquired.

"I shall be dressed as Toby Peters, Detective."

"There is only room for one detective at this party, and it shall be Salvador Dali. There is a costume for you in your room and one for the poet. Gala picked them. She can see through to the soul."

I was about to say no again, but Dali wouldn't let me get started.

"No one goes to the shore without wearing a mask of the gods."

Depending on what torture Gala had laid out on the bed, it wasn't such a bad idea to be in some kind of disguise. There wasn't much chance of the L.A. cops showing up, but there was a chance the killer would come. That chance became a near certainty about ten minutes after the thought hit me.

The phone rang in the kitchen. Nobody paid attention. I picked it up. Over the clattering of the caterers and

Gala's shouting, a falsetto voice said, "Peters: Tonight, when the sun goes down, the painting will be revealed and Salvador Dali will face his punishment."

Whoever it was hung up. I looked around to see if Dali was there or Gala was paying attention. They weren't.

I went looking for Jeremy to tell him about the call and found him in the bedroom. He was wearing a toga with a gold rope around his waist.

"I am to be Plato."

"You don't have to do it, Jeremy."

"I don't mind. When I wrestled, I learned to accept costume and performance."

I looked at the other costume on the bed. It was brown with leather shorts and with a little feathered hat, boots and a bow, and a quiver full of arrows.

"What's that?"

"William Tell," said Jeremy. "You have been honored. William Tell is Dali's favorite character."

"Why?"

Jeremy shrugged. Somehow, his shrug looked more meaningful in a toga.

"Tell is the archetypal father whose child's life is in his hands. The child is dependent on the skill and courage of the father. Life and death, skill and faith. The child's fate is in the hands of the father."

"My knees'll show," I said, picking up the shorts.

"When you wear a bathing suit, they show," Jeremy said gently.

"I don't wear a bathing suit. I don't go to the beach."

"Tonight you will," he reminded me, and I told him about the phone call.

11

Even before the sun was fully down there were four fires on the beach, blazes in giant copper pots. Dali supervised each one personally. Jeremy and I watched from the top of the hill where we could see down the beach for about a hundred yards in both directions. Dali was a frantic ball of white fur, cracking orders to hired hands who tended the fires. He ran from pot to pot like a vaudeville juggler trying to keep plates spinning on wobbly sticks.

In the center of the fiery pots, its heavy legs sinking into the sand, was the throne. Every once in a while Dali paused in his steeplechase to be sure the throne hadn't gotten up on its legs and dashed into the ocean. Two long tables filled with seafood—lobsters, clams, shrimp, scallops—sat right on the shoreline where the tide was sure to get them in a few hours.

"I think he plans to let the sea take the food later," Jeremy said.

"Looks that way," I agreed, trying to reach a particularly itchy spot under my William Tell shorts. I couldn't get at it, so I tried to do it with an arrow. I was reasonably successful.

The second set of guests arrived: a snail and an orange. Gala, dressed like a Cossack complete with tunic, fur cap, and beard, stood at the top of the sandy trail and pointed them toward the beach. At Gala's request, Jeremy had carried the big clock outside and it stood next to her.

After Gala and the clock greeted each guest, they had to go past Jeremy and me, and we stopped them.

"I'm an orange," the orange said.

"I can see that," I said.

"Don't shoot me," he went on.

The snail roared with laughter.

"Get it?" said the snail. "William Tell shoots apples, not oranges."

"Sorry," I said to the orange. "We've got to frisk you for contraband."

The snail thought this was funny, too, but the orange started to protest.

"Dali's orders," I said with a shrug and a look intended to make them think that it was just another eccentricity of the master.

I think the orange finally shrugged. I don't know. The snail, even though she was a lady, was easier to search than the orange. We stood back and watched the couple waddle down the hill. I said, "Jeremy, this isn't going to work."

Looking particularly wise in his toga, he replied, "We will do what must be done."

What had to be done next was to confront a woman in a gown and a head full of snakes instead of hair. The snakes looked too damned real.

"The Gorgon," said Jeremy.

The man with her, if you ignored his big belly, looked

like a Greek soldier complete with a big shiny shield. I tried to get under his armor. He was ticklish.

"Perseus," Jeremy explained as the couple staggered down the hill. "He could only look at the Gorgon in his shield lest he turn to stone."

They started to come too quickly for us to keep up with them. A herd of masked lemmings going over the cliff toward the water, lemmings disguised as ballerinas in fishing boots, buffaloes with the heads of owls, giant polka-dot chicken legs, red satin robots, and a hooded monk or executioner with ax. There were men dressed like women and women dressed like men. Half-man half-two-headed-horses, a bottle of mustard with an elephant's trunk, and something that could have been a big wrinkled chili bean. It could have been something else, too, but I preferred to think it was a chili bean.

The noise level had risen considerably, though the waves were still slapping loud and close.

An angel and a Catholic priest wearing lipstick and sporting a long tail were the last to join the party. The angel, with white gown and feather wings, stopped next to us, played a few notes on her harp, and announced, "There should be no fires on the beach. The Japanese. It will draw the Japanese."

"I think he plans to lure them to the beach and then pelt them with live lobsters," I said.

"Droll," commented the priest, heading down the hill to give her blessings.

"You hear that, Jeremy, it's droll."

"An essence of Surrealism is its offense," Jeremy said.

"Anything?" asked Gala the Cossack, coming to our side and looking down at the madness on the beach. "Anything suspicious, strange?"

I looked down at the sight below, a beach full of escapees from a casting call for *Dante's Inferno* or *Freaks*.

"Looks normal to me," I said.

"Dali seems pleased," she said, stroking her beard. "Please bring down the clock."

She headed down the sandy path toward her husband, who was standing on the seat of the throne, his paws folded, a mad knowing smile on his face.

"I'm going down, Jeremy," I said, picking up the clock. "Keep an eye on things from up here."

"It's a bacchanal," he said. "An astounding vision. If I had paper and a pen I'd write a poem."

"Togas don't have pockets," I reminded him.

"I like that," he said. "That will be the title of the poem, 'Togas Don't Have Pockets'—a surreal title for a surreal poem."

The bow hooked over my shoulder dug into my back and the clock sank its claws into my stomach as I scurried down the hill and moved next to Dali on his throne in time to hear a woman dressed like a man say, "I hope you don't die like the other painters, just when I get interested in your work."

"In that case," said Dali, "I hope we are both fortunate enough for me to outlive you."

The woman backed away with a happy smile, and Dali leaned down to me and told me to place the clock before him on a marble pedestal. His voice was panicky as he put a paw on my shoulder: "They are coming too close and the sea is beginning to whisper something to me."

"How about we call it a night and send the circus home early?" I suggested.

"Early? Early is dawn. The night is just coming. Fire dances in the waves. A feast of cannibals. Look. The lobsters look alive in their hands. Holes will appear in their flesh."

"Sounds like fun to me," I said.

"This," contradicted Dali, "is not fun. This is art. Critics lurk beneath the masks, ready to steal my soul.

Buyers hide their hideous drool behind hoods. They want to gather in my paintings, devour them in private feasts behind closed doors. *Vampiros.* Is that a real priest?"

"I hope not," I said.

A voice rose from somewhere behind us. I couldn't tell if it was a man or a woman.

"You could never be my analyst, Roland. You are not truly literate."

The snail appeared with a polka-dot chicken leg, stage whispering, "His paintings reveal so much of the Id that one can but anticipate with longing his return to consciousness."

"Quiet," shouted Gala, who suddenly appeared on the throne next to her furry husband. Her arms were raised high and her slight voice fought the ocean and the murmuring of the guests. Behind her, Dali adjusted his deerstalker, folded his arms, and turned his chin up in a pose uncomfortably like one of Mussolini's. "At midnight, Dali will wind the clock and time will begin. But first, he will recite a poem of love and honor."

The crowd went silent except for the orange, who had turned into a giant screwdriver—the vodka kind—and was babbling about hairy teeth.

"Off with his head," Dali ordered the executioner, pointing at the offending fruit.

The executioner weaved through the crowd and headed for the orange, who saw him coming, screamed, and went running up the beach in the general direction of Monterey. With relative calm restored, Dali began to recite in a language that sounded a little like Spanish, but just a little.

The bottle of mustard whispered, "I think it's Portuguese."

"No," said a small voice behind me. "It is Catalan."

"Gunther," I said, turning around to look down at the Coroner of the Munchkins.

"It was all I could find at short notice," he said.

Gala glared down at us with a look to whither knaves, and Dali went on gesturing eloquently as he continued reciting and pointing at the sea.

"What are you doing here?" I whispered to Gunther.

"The phone here is disconnected and I had to tell you—" he began, but Dali stopped him.

"You have come from a dream to destroy my poetry," Dali shouted.

"On the contrary," said Gunther, who was not known to possess a sense of humor. "We have come from Los Angeles in time to save your life."

"We?" I asked.

"I drove here with Alice Pallis and the baby Natasha," Gunther explained.

The crowd on the beach applauded. They seemed to think the Munchkin and the archer were part of the performance.

"Minute impostor," Dali cried. "You destroyed my poem. You try to frighten Dali."

"You were reciting 'Goldilocks and the Three Bears' in Catalan," said Gunther.

Dali looked astounded. Tears welled in his eyes. His mustaches wilted.

"Off with his head," cried Gala.

The executioner made his way back from the shore and advanced on Gunther. The crowd loved it. A zebra-striped onion on my right began to weep with laughter.

"It is the Three Bears," Gunther repeated with dignity.

The executioner shouldered his ax, reached down, and picked Gunther up under one arm.

"Priceless," cackled the snail.

I put my arm on the executioner's shoulder. "Put him down."

The executioner shook me off and started up the hill with Gunther struggling to get free. I went after them and tripped on my bow.

"Brilliant," shouted a man behind me.

"Bravo," called another.

I didn't look back but I had the feeling Dali was either taking a bow and credit or curling into a ball and crying. I looked to the top of the hill for Jeremy, but he wasn't there so I scrambled forward.

The executioner with his Munchkin bundle had disappeared around a corner of the house by the time I made it to the top and managed to stand. I moved none-too-quickly after them and knew when I turned the corner that I was going to lose the race.

My hope was that the executioner was one of Dali's hirelings or pals. My fear was that he was Gregory Novak. There were cars in front of the house on the driveway and on the unpaved street, but no executioner with a Munchkin. I considered putting an arrow in my bow and stalking through the forest of cars, but I didn't have much faith in my bow or my aim.

I wondered where Jeremy was, but I didn't take time to look for him. Instead I went back to the house and opened the door. Something clattered. The lights were all on, which didn't make me feel any better. I expected the big guy with the hood to come out from behind everything with ax raised high. But Gunther was in trouble, so I moved forward, considering possible weapons. The best I could do was a stone figure of a naked woman on a shelf. The woman figure looked like a garden rake with big round eyes.

I followed the clatter to the room Jeremy and I had slept in. From the hallway I couldn't see anyone in the bedroom. I didn't want to take any chances, at least any more than I could avoid. I was about to step into the room when something soft and fuzzy touched my hand.

I think I yelped. I turned and started to swing at a startled Sherlock Rabbit whose mustaches went wild.

"*Assassino*," cried Dali.

I didn't have time or the chance to reply because the blade of an ax came whistling past my ear and tore through the wall next to my face. I pushed Dali into the room ahead of me and took a swing over my shoulder with the big-eyed rake woman. I hit the hooded guy on the shoulder. I turned to face him and try again, but he had already pulled the ax out of the wall and was ready for another go at me.

I ran. Dali was ahead of me. I shoved him through a door and kicked it closed behind me.

"Run," I said. "Get help."

There was a latch on the door. I threw it just as the executioner turned the handle. Dali watched, mouth open. He didn't run.

The ax head came crashing through the door, straight through and missed my nose, which is fortunately so flat that it's almost no nose, by the width of a War stamp.

I pushed Dali into the next room. I slammed the door shut behind us. It didn't have a lock. I picked up a chair and shoved it under the door handle.

This, as you may recall, is about where I started the story. So let's leap forward about a minute.

There I sit behind the driver's seat in my little green hat with a red feather, Dali next to me, a cowering bunny with a rapidly wilting mustache.

In front of me, through the windshield, I could see a hole in the little tin hood of my Crosley. Behind, in the mirror, I could see trees. Beside me, just outside the window, the executioner pulled the ax back. There was no room to move. There is no forward or backward in a

Crosley and Dali filled what little there was on my right.
"Open the goddamn door and run, Sal." I ordered.

I closed my eyes, expected the crash of glass, shards across my face, even the blade digging into my skull. I heard the door open and Dali gasp. Something was happening just outside the window. I opened my eyes and beheld on the hood of the Crosley, gurgling at me, a beautiful smiling baby. I turned to look at the executioner and saw him stagger back, a hand grabbing the wrist of his ax-arm, another hand pulling back the executioner's hood.

I shoved Dali through the far door and scrambled after him. We turned to watch the battle. But it wasn't much of a battle. The executioner was big and strong, but Alice Pallis was stronger. Jeremy appeared from the side of the house and ran forward to scoop his daughter from the hood of the Crosley just as Alice lifted the executioner and threw him over the top of the car. The ax sailed out of his hand and through a window at the back of the house.

"Thanks, Alice," I said. Jeremy handed his wife the baby.

Dali looked down at the executioner.

"Odelle!"

Odelle, a cut the size of the Russian River on her forehead, looked up at Dali with hatred.

Jeremy lifted Odelle up and sat her on the hood of my Crosley. The hood sagged. From the beach we could hear what sounded like the chant of monks.

"Where's Gunther?" I demanded, grabbing her shoulder.

"Gunther?" asked a dazed Odelle.

"The little guy."

"In the house," she mumbled. "I locked him in a closet."

"Why did you want to kill Dali?" Dali asked, completely bewildered.

"Betrayer," came Odelle's reply.

"You are mad," he said.

"I have the painting," she said between tightly clenched teeth as blood rivered down her face. "You had my faith, my loyalty, and you were laughing at me."

"Never," said Dali, looking to me, Jeremy, Alice, and baby Natasha for support. Since we didn't know what the hell they were talking about, we stood watching.

"Why'd you kill them?" I asked her.

"Them?" Odelle asked, looking at me.

"Street, Place, Taylor," I said.

"The only one I killed was Taylor, in his kitchen. He wanted to sell the painting back. He was going to give it to Dali for money. I wanted to destroy Dali and then his reputation. I won't cry."

Alice shifted the baby and came up with a handkerchief.

"Wipe your face," Alice said gently and Odelle wiped her face.

"Taylor killed Street and Place?" I tried.

"No," she said. "They were dead before he got to them."

"Then who the hell killed Street and Place?"

No one answered; then I remembered.

"Gunther."

"Gunther killed them?" asked Alice.

"No," I said. "Gunther he knew who killed them."

I pushed past Dali and ran into the house through broken doors, around overturned furniture. It wasn't hard to find Gunther. He was kicking at the door of the closet of the room where Jeremy and I had slept. I opened the door and the Munchkin coroner came tumbling out. I helped him up and led him to the nearest bed.

"You all right, Gunther?"

"I am all right," he said, looking around to see if anyone but me was present to view his loss of dignity.

"Alice caught the executioner who threw you in the closet," I said.

"It was a woman."

"Right," I said. "She says she didn't kill Street or Place. You said . . ."

"Grigory Yefimovich Novykh," said Gunther.

"Grig . . . Gregory Novak?"

"No," corrected Gunther, removing his hat and placing it on the bed. "Grigory Yefimovich Novykh, the son of Yefim Novykh born in Pokroyvskoye, Russia, where as a boy he was given the name by which he would be known throughout his life—the Debaucher, or, in Russian, Rasputin. Your Misters Place and Street were murdered by Rasputin."

12

Rasputin died twenty-six years ago in St. Petersburg," Jeremy said, entering the room with baby Natasha in his arms.

"He died in Florida?" I asked.

"St. Petersburg, Russia. Leningrad," Jeremy explained.

"A dead man killed Place and Street?" I asked, reasonably.

"Alice has taken the lady to see a doctor," Jeremy went on. "She'll then take her to the police. Dali went back to his party."

"The painting, the one you told me to keep, the one with the hole shot in it," said Gunther, removing his fake beard. "The clock."

"A painting of one of the clocks," I confirmed.

"There was writing on the clock in the painting. Is there writing in Russian on the bottom of the clocks?"

"Yes," I said, "but what's . . . ?"

"The writing says, 'I place a curse on these clocks,

which I leave for Yusupov, Purishkevich, Pavlovich, and Lazovert. I remind them that time will end and they will join me where time has no beginning.' And it is signed, 'Rasputin.'"

"A curse killed Place and Street, a curse on some clocks by a dead . . . whatever he was," I said, walking to the window.

"He was a mystic, a Siberian peasant, who apparently improved the condition of Alexis Nikolayevich, the hemophiliac heir to the Russian throne," said Jeremy.

I wasn't about to argue with a giant in a toga. Natasha started to make a humming sound. Jeremy bounced her gently in his arms and kept talking.

"He became an adviser to the Empress Alexandra and preached that sin was a necessary prerequisite to salvation. The Empress was convinced that this sexually obsessed holy man could not only save her son but also the Romanov dynasty, and the Russian autocracy. When World War I began, rumors of his having an affair with the Empress were accepted as truth, and just before the war a group of men—a prince, a physician, a member of the Duma, the legislature, and the Grand Duke—decided to kill Rasputin. There is reason to believe that Rasputin was aware of their plan but felt they would not dare to kill him. On the night of December 30—actually December 17 on the old Russian calendar—the doctor poisoned Rasputin. He did not die so the Prince shot him, but Rasputin ran and the member of the Duma shot him again. They then tied him up and threw him in the Neva River. An examination of the body showed that Rasputin drowned."

"You want me to guess the names of the four guys who killed Rasputin?" I asked.

"Feliks Yusupov, Vladimir Mitrofamonov Purishkevich, Dmitry Pavlovich, and Dr. Lazovert," Jeremy supplied.

"Dr. Lazovert," I said. "I heard . . . He was a friend of Gala's family. She mentioned him or someone with a name like that when she . . ."

"Time?" asked Jeremy.

I looked at my father's watch. It said six-twenty, which may have been true in Paris, but not in Carmel.

"Midnight," said Gunther, examining the pocket watch he pulled out from under his black tunic.

Jeremy handed me the baby and ran for the door with Gunther a few steps behind him. I followed them, cursing my healing leg, and got to the hill overlooking the beach in time to see first Jeremy and then Gunther hit the bottom and race across the sand toward Gala and Dali, who stood in front of the clock surrounded by the odd crowd.

Jeremy was shouting, but no one was listening. His toga dragged behind him. Crazy shadows from the bonfires danced on the side of the hill and along the sand. At midnight, Dali had said, his wife would wind the clock.

I tried yelling, but it was no use. Jeremy hit the crowd as Gala held up the key to the clock and said something I couldn't make out, something in Russian. I had the feeling she was reciting the words written on the bottom of the clock. Her hand came down and the key approached the hole in the clock face. Dali stood triumphant on his throne, his hand on his wife's shoulder. Jeremy was almost there. He was approaching from behind the Dalis. I suppose his idea was to stop Gala, but I could see there was no time.

Natasha chewed on my nose as Gala turned the key and the guests screamed and cheered.

Jeremy was at her side now. He shoved her toward the ocean as a bullet blasted out of the clock. Jeremy's hand shot back as if it had been punched by Joe Louis.

The crowd stepped back. Screams. Shouts. One or two

vegetables and a woman-man laughed. Gunther leaped onto the throne next to Dali, who put his hands over his eyes. Gunther ripped a piece from his coroner's cloak and grabbed Jeremy's bleeding hand. From where Natasha and I stood watching her father, he showed no sign of the pain he must have been feeling.

Dali jumped from the throne, took a quick look at his wife to be sure she was all right, and draped Jeremy's uninjured arm around his shoulder. Gala took the other and together they helped Jeremy up the hill to where Natasha and I stood waiting.

Natasha reached for her father and Jeremy removed his good hand from Dali's shoulder to take her.

"We'll get you to a doctor, Jeremy," I assured him.

"We will get him to the finest surgeon in the world," proclaimed Salvador Dali.

"An emergency room will be fine," said Jeremy. "I received a much more severe laceration when Carl 'the Monster' Frisson bit me during our match in Montreal in 1926."

"My car is here," said Gunther. "I will take him."

"You'll probably run into Alice and Odelle," I said. "Sal, you're standing in the grass."

"So?" said Dali, a paw aimed at the ground.

"Grasshoppers," I reminded him.

Dali laughed.

"Salvador Dali laughs at grasshoppers," he said. "Monks have chased Dali with axes. Clocks have attacked his Gala. I will immortalize this moment. Gala will be depicted as a martyr. Dali will eat grasshoppers and laugh at the Metro."

"I've got a question," I said, turning to Gala. "You're Russian. The curse on the clocks is in Russian. Why didn't you . . . ?"

"Nonsense, superstitious nonsense," she said. "I knew

the curse was put there to increase the value of the clocks."

I was going to point out that in this case the curse had been real, that two people had died because of it and she had come close to being the third victim, but she was on to another topic.

"The painting," said Gala, pulling at her husband's white furry arm. "The third painting."

"Yes," Dali said, suddenly sober as we watched Gunther and Jeremy amble into the darkness.

Dali turned to look down the hill at what was left of his party. The bonfires were dying on the beach and the crowd had thinned to a few shadows. One of the tables had been carried out by the tide and waves and lay on its side half out of the water. The other table tottered with each wave, and the last of the food slid off into the surf.

"You know where Odelle lives?" I asked.

"A house, not far from here," said Gala. "She lived with her mother till her mother died last year. The house is on Lotus Street. Three streets that way, then left, a blue wooden house."

"Let's go," I said. "We can all squeeze into my car."

"I will stay here," said Gala.

I could see that Dali didn't want to go without her, but she urged him to turn and go with me. I wanted to change clothes. I wanted him to change clothes, but I didn't want him to take time to think. The Crosley was battered but it ran.

The house was a little bungalow about two minutes away, inland, on a street just off of what passed for downtown Carmel. There was a light on inside. We walked down the sidewalk to the front door, a battered William Tell and Sherlock Bunny after midnight.

The door was open. This was Carmel. People still left their doors open. I knew that was changing everywhere.

We entered the living room, a small, neat box of a room

with old sun-faded furniture on spindly legs that didn't look as if they could support Odelle. There was a Dali painting on the wall. I didn't see anything different about it. Nude woman on the left, her back half turned. Some figures in heavy black dresses in the middle, under some rotting stone arches. A desert in the background. Hills, sky.

Dali saw me examining the painting.

"A reproduction," he pronounced with distaste. "Dali disdains reproductions. Paint must have dimension."

We moved past the tiny lighted kitchen into the only other room in the house, a bedroom with an unmade oversized bed. Above the bed was a big painting of a woman with two babies in her arms. I looked around and headed for the closet in the corner.

"Where are you going?" Dali asked.

"It might be in there," I said.

"No," said Dali. "Dali has changed his mind. He no longer wants to find the painting."

"*Changed his* . . . well, Toby Peters has *not* changed his mind. I lost my hood, got clobbered by a state cop, almost fell off a tower, and came close to losing my head to find that painting. I'm finding it. Tell Salvador Dali when you see him."

"It is not in the closet." Dali's round eyes were opened wide and moist. His mustaches were drooping and in need of a quick fix of wax.

"How do you know till we . . ." I began, but he pointed at the painting of the woman and two babies over the bed.

I looked at the picture again and understood why Dali was afraid of having the public discover his secret painting. There was nothing surreal about it. It looked almost like one of the religious paintings in *National Geographic*, a madonna and child, only this was two babies. The mother, obviously posed by Odelle, looked down at them: two naked, smiling boys.

"That is my mother," said Dali, his eyes wet with tears. "And that is me and my brother, who died before I was born. We were both named Salvador Dali."

"I like it," I said.

"Sentimental romanticism," said Dali softly. "My enemies would crucify me, call me a fraud. My paintings, those in the other room, come from the dungeons of my soul. This one comes from my heart. The world must never know that Salvador Dali has a heart. If the world knows that Salvador Dali has a heart, enemies will come and eat it."

There was a washroom off the bedroom. Dali disappeared into it. I heard the water running and then he came out holding a sopping washcloth in his paw. He stepped up on the bed and stood in front of the painting for a moment, took a deep breath, and attacked his signature in the lower left-hand corner.

I could hear his breath coming in little gasps as he raised the cloth in front of the face of the little boy on the left. His hand swayed.

"I cannot," he said.

"Your name's not on it anymore."

"But there are those who would know," he said.

"I've got an idea. I'll cut my fee in half and you give me the painting. I'll hang it in my office. No one's going to believe it's a Dali, not in my office."

Dali put the washcloth in his mouth and sucked it while he thought. When he removed it, a small blotch of orange paint showed on his right cheek.

"Take it," he said with a great sigh. "Take it. Perhaps one day I shall visit it. Perhaps one day when I do not worry so much about the vulnerability of my heart I will clasp it to my soul."

"Makes sense to me," I said, getting on the bed and lifting the painting down.

We had to cover the painting with a blanket from Odelle's bed and tie it to the top of the Crosley with some drapery cords we found in a closet. It wanted to slither down the windshield at first, but I eventually had it secured.

On the way back to his house, Dali spoke only once:

"Very few people know who I am. And I am not one of them."

13

We caravaned home to Los Angeles. Alice drove one car, with Jeremy and Natasha in the back seat. Gunther drove alone in his giant black Daimler, and I led the way in my massacred Crosley. Odelle was in the Monterey jail waiting for an L.A. cop to come and bring her back to book her for Taylor's murder.

Gala had paid me in cash. I told her I wanted to submit a bill, that I had all the notes, that I would cut it in half and wait for payment but she declined.

"No, we put an end. Dali must put an end."

We settled on $130, plus the painting. With the $500 from Barry Zeman, I now had $630.

I led the way in case I had a breakdown. The breakdown threatened but never quite came and I chugged into No-Neck Arnie's with Gunther right behind. Jeremy, Alice, and Natasha had headed back to the Farraday.

"Vehicle is dead," said Arnie, rubbing his hands on his overalls. "What happened?"

"Executioner came after it with an ax," I said.

"That'll ruin 'em every time," he said.

Gunther drove me to the Farraday and waited while I went upstairs, and put the Dali painting in my office. It filled an entire wall and covered some cracks that needed covering. Shelly was nowhere around. There were some phone messages scrawled by Shelly and punctured on the metal spindle on the desk. I called Phil's house and a woman answered. I didn't recognize the voice.

"This is Toby," I said, looking at the phone messages. "Phil's brother."

"I'm Mrs. Dudnick. Nathan and David said you were coming to take them to a movie after school, but Mr. Pevsner told the boys not to expect you."

"I'll be there, Mrs. Dudnick," I said, seeing that another message was from my ex-wife, Anne. "How's Ruth?"

"Surgery was this morning. Haven't heard yet."

"Thanks," I said. "I'll be over at four to pick up the boys."

The third message on the spindle read: *Woman called. Said she was Greta Garbo. Will call back.*

Shelly was seated in his dental chair doing a dental crossword puzzle in one of his journals when I came out.

"When did the Garbo call come, Shel?"

"Six-letter word for 'tooth rot,'" he mulled.

"The Garbo call," I repeated.

"Lousy imitation," Shelly said, looking up from his puzzle and launching into awful Garbo. "I vant to be by mineself."

"'To be alone,' Shel. She didn't say 'mineself.'"

"Mineself. Alone. Whatever. Well?" he asked.

"Well?" I answered.

"The tooth. Dali was supposed to paint me a tooth, remember?"

"I guess he forgot. He had a lot on his mind."

Shelly put his magazine in his lap, pulled out a cigar, lit it and thought for a few seconds before saying, "Can't trust artists or hardware store clerks."

I wanted to call Anne but it would have to wait. I went downstairs, got into Gunther's car and asked him to drive me to the hospital. It took about fifteen minutes. We got there just after noon, and my stomach was growling.

"I'll meet you back at Mrs. Plaut's," I said. "Thanks for everything, Gunther."

"I am pleased to have been of service," he said, looking clean-shaven and spiffy in his powder blue suit complete with matching vest.

I found Phil in the surgery waiting room, his tie loose, his eyes red.

"How is she, Phil?" I asked, sitting next to him.

He looked at me and shook his head as if remembering some long-ago stupid question I had asked him.

"She'll be okay," he said. "Doctor said it looks like she'll be okay. Goddamn doctors."

"Goddamn doctors," I agreed.

"You trying to be funny?" he asked, turning to me, his fists tight, ready. He needed a shave.

"No," I said. "I'm not trying to be funny. You want to go get something to eat?"

"No," he said.

We sat in silence for about three minutes, looking at the door, waiting for a nurse, a doctor, a report.

"You're still wanted for taking evidence from the scene of a crime," he said.

"I didn't kill that guy, Phil. You know I—"

"I know. I heard. Some shit about clocks and dead guys committing murder. It's Cawelti's case. I don't want to hear about it."

"How about when we hear about Ruth we go out for something to eat and go back to my office?"

"Back to your office?" Phil said, looking at me with red eyes. "Why the hell would I want to go to your office?"

"I bought a painting," I said. "Mother and two kids. Looks like you and me and Mom."

"What have you been drinking, Tobias? Mom died when you were born. You didn't even know her."

I didn't say anything.

"Hell," Phil said suddenly, running his thick right hand over his short-cropped white hair, "Let's go look at your painting."

My brother punched my shoulder and we both stood up. I looked down at my father's watch.

"Quarter after one," I said.

Phil looked at his watch.

"Quarter after one," he agreed.

THE
END